VERDICT: LOVE

A Tennessee: Love Romance

VERDICT: LOVE

•

Donna Wright

AVALON BOOKS
NEW YORK

Published by Thomas Bouregy & Co., Inc.
160 Madison Avenue, New York, NY 10016

Library of Congress Cataloging-in-Publication Data

Wright, Donna (Donna A.)
    Verdict : love / Donna Wright.
        p. cm. — (Tennessee love romance series)
        ISBN 978-0-8034-9855-6 (acid-free paper)
    1. Tennessee—Fiction.   I. Title.

    PS3623.R5344V47 2007
    813'.6—dc22

                                    2007016631

PRINTED IN THE UNITED STATES OF AMERICA
ON ACID-FREE PAPER
BY HADDON CRAFTSMEN, BLOOMSBURG, PENNSYLVANIA

For David

Chapter One

"**D**on't you dare even *think* about it!" Kendra shouted.

"That thing is wild!" her neighbor yelled back at her. "And I'm a hunter!" He waved toward his camouflage pants and shirt, as if his wardrobe made the point for him.

Kendra Simms ran, carrot in hand, toward the little potbellied pig. The woods behind the subdivision where she and her mother lived had become a place where people often dropped off unwanted pets, and this pig appeared to be another such stray.

"It's not wild! You can tell from its size, it's one of those pet ones." She'd noticed the little pig snuffling around the trees for at least a

1

month now but had never been able to get close to it.

"Well, if you ask me, it could be one of those canned hams. *They* must come from small hogs."

Len Hicks had never been the brightest bulb in the pack, but this was too much.

"If you don't put that gun down, I'm calling the cops."

The words were no more out of her mouth than a patrol car pulled up in front of her neighbor's home, lights flashing.

A policeman exited the car and gazed up the hill where Kendra and her nemesis faced each other. "You doing okay up there, Len?"

Great. They know each other.

Kendra eyed them both, then spoke to the officer. "Your pal, *Len,* is trying to kill this little pig."

The officer met them where they stood and gazed around the area. "What little pig?"

A cursory glance told Kendra that the object of the conflict had moved to a less crowded space.

Or so she thought. After a few seconds a pink flash moved past her and ran straight through the officer's legs. She followed it in a dive. The officer fell backward, but not before she and the pig had scrambled far enough away from him to avoid being hurt.

"Here, piggy, piggy, piggy." Her words were little more than grunts as she crawled toward the animal, holding out the carrot, twigs breaking beneath her as she moved.

The pig glared at her as it backed away slowly. But the carrot gave Kendra an advantage. She stopped moving. The pig quit backing away, its eyes darting from the people to the bribe.

She heard a gun cock, so she rolled over quickly and kicked upward, knocking the rifle from Len's hands.

It went off in midair, scaring the pig, who scuttled away in a second. The gun twirled in the air like a baton before it hit the ground.

Slowly Kendra pulled herself to her feet. "You idiot! You could have killed someone. Me, for instance! What in the world were you thinking?"

She leaned over and helped the officer up. "You okay?"

His gaze sheepishly met hers. "I'm fine. But getting stuck in the leg with a carrot and knocked down by a pig isn't going to look good in my report."

"What? What about Len, here? He shot at me!"

"I did not! I shot at that stupid pig. I'd have gotten him, too, if you hadn't interfered. You saw it, Bert. You saw how she acted."

Not only were they friends, but the cop glanced at his pal as if he agreed with him.

Kendra couldn't believe it. "With all the houses in this area, you discharged a weapon. That has to count for something on the books."

"Well . . ." Hicks stammered, "you . . . you . . . you attacked an officer of the law."

The policeman brightened, maybe envisioning a better report to write.

"That is not true. I tried to catch the pig. That's all." She spun around to the officer. "You know what happened."

"All I know is I was knocked down, and now I'm covered in dirt. If you'll turn around, miss, you're under arrest for assaulting a police officer."

She braced herself. "I'm not taking part in this farce."

"Ma'am, put your hands behind your back, and drop the carrot."

She crossed her arms over her chest. "I will do no such thing."

He pulled his cuffs from his belt. "I've asked you nicely to drop the carrot."

She didn't move.

"This is your final warning, miss. Drop the carrot."

"Walter, there's no way I'm prosecuting Kendra Simms again." Hugh Cramer towered over the District Attorney of White County in the man's office. He threw the file onto his desk. Boss or no boss, Hugh wasn't taking any more nonsense from Walter.

The older, slightly balding man didn't want to hear Hugh's protests. "You'll prosecute the offenders I assign you, Cramer. That's what you're here for."

Hugh drew in a long breath and sat down. "We're both adults. Let's just say it and be done with it. When I came here, you thought I'd hate this and go back to defense."

"You're right, I did."

"I win cases, Walter. I put the bad guys behind bars. Isn't that what you want?"

The other man leaned forward. "I want you to look me in the eye and tell me you're not after my job."

Hugh put his hands up, as if surrendering. "Easily enough done. Politics are the cause of every problem in the civilized world. I won't run for DA. Now are you happy?"

Walter sat back. "You prosecute this case, then we'll talk again."

Hugh pressed his index finger onto the file. "I don't want this case. That's why I'm here. This woman is a menace to this office, not to society."

"I think that's my call."

Hugh could see he was getting nowhere. "Fine. We'll have the circus, then."

He stormed out of his boss's office and down the hall to his own small cubby of a work area. He kept thinking how different things were on his mother's favorite lawyer shows. He shook his head as he thought of their conversation last night. She really expected him to conquer the world now that he'd crossed over to the prosecution. Of course, he knew her only reference was a popular television series; he himself hadn't anticipated such master-of-the universe nonsense. Still, their chat had made him think. He could have stayed on the other side of the fence, made more money, and not had to put up with Walter Henry, District Attorney for White County.

Of course, everything had a downside, even the defense. Lose a case, and the convict plots a murder the whole time he's racking up the years. And the murder is of the lawyer who didn't get him off, even though the assailant was caught holding the smoking gun in one hand and the jewelry he'd stolen in the other.

Sheesh.

His secretary made him a cup of coffee and sat down opposite him. "How'd it go?"

Hugh snorted. "I still have the case, if that's what you're asking."

"You need to be at her arraignment at nine. You've got half an hour. And don't make that face at my coffee. At least it's free, and someone else made it."

"Lydia, you know I love you. But when it's your turn to make the coffee, people go home sick." He grabbed the file and tossed it into his open briefcase.

Lydia walked from his office. "You need to count to ten."

"More like twenty." He slammed the case shut. "I can't believe this."

Hugh fumed on his walk to the courthouse for Kendra Simms' arraignment. No one could frustrate him the way that woman could. Okay, so she was beautiful and smart and had a good cause, but she could be so irresponsible, and she got into more trouble than a cat in a dog pound.

He walked into the courtroom just as Judge Cole entered.

The bailiff shouted a little more loudly than was necessary, "All rise! The Honorable Judge Thomas Cole presiding over this court."

Cole stared at the bailiff a long moment, as if to ask where he'd gotten a megaphone.

A little less as if he was at a football game, the bailiff announced, "First case, docket number 172705, the People versus Kendra J. Simms, assaulting a police officer." He handed the judge a folder.

Kendra Simms moved from one of the benches in the room to the lectern for the defense.

Alone.

The judge waited a moment, then asked, "Miss Simms, who is the lucky attorney representing you today?"

"According to the law I can represent myself. That's what I plan to do."

Hugh closed his eyes but could only get to five in his silent count before the judge banged his gavel to hush the murmurings in the room.

Miss Affirmative Defense even pulled a gigantic book from a huge canvas bag. "Your Honor, I do have that right." She opened the legal text.

Not wanting to hear any more, Hugh rolled

his eyes. "I don't deny that Miss Simms can represent herself, Judge Cole. Everyone knows that's the law. We don't need her to point it out to us." Hugh shook his head as he stared straight at the root of his problems. "However, as we also know, the man—or woman, in this case—who represents herself has a fool for a client."

Chuckles could be heard throughout the courtroom.

The judged glared at the spectators, the people waiting to be arraigned, and the lawyers ready to represent them. "Don't make me clear this courtroom," he warned.

Miss Simms huffed, pushing her dark hair over her delicate shoulders. "I am no fool. I know the laws in these matters better than anyone."

"As well you should," Hugh scoffed. "You've broken all of them."

The judge smiled—despite himself, it seemed. "I have no choice but to move forward, counselor." To Kendra he said, "How do you plead?"

"Not guilty, Your Honor."

The judge asked, "Where do you stand on bail, Mr. Cramer?"

Hugh found his opening. "Your Honor, it's apparent, as many times as Miss Simms has been before this court, that she feels the laws of our town county don't apply to her. Although I would concede that she is not a flight risk, I think it's time the court asked her to put her money where her so-called beliefs are. We ask for twenty-thousand dollars' bail."

Miss Simms' mouth fell open as she turned from him to the judge.

Before she could speak, the judge waved her protest away. He taunted Hugh with a wry grin. "A little high, counselor."

"I know. I ask this only because it's time that the example set by Miss Simms is dealt with appropriately."

The judge scratched his chin in thought.

Good.

Miss Simms began to speak rapidly, nervously. "Your Honor, really. I didn't kill anyone—"

The judge interrupted. "No, but this time you *did* knock down a policeman."

"I can easily prove that that charge was blown way out of proportion."

"That's for a jury to decide. Bail is set at five . . ." He paused, then added, ". . . hundred dollars. I'll see you two on March 27. Miss Simms, I suggest you find representation." He banged his gavel. "Next case."

Hugh grabbed his briefcase and smiled to himself as he walked from the courtroom.

Fifteen minutes later, as he left the courthouse, someone caught him by the arm. He turned to face Kendra Simms.

"You, Hugh Cramer, are the most pigheaded man I've ever known," she spouted.

"Excuse me, Miss Simms, but I take exception to that description."

"You think you're so good, with that big bail you tried to get in there, but I'll bury you in court," she ranted.

He hated to grin right in her face. On second thought, no, he didn't. "I thought you might want to plead this one out."

"Plead it out? The cop's friend fired a gun at a pig that was running loose in the woods behind our house. When I tried to rescue the little guy, the police officer was somehow . . . knocked over. You can't make this one stick, Cramer."

Her eyes flashed the prettiest green when she was in fight mode.

"I think if you're going to be your own attorney, you'd better do some research. Assaulting a police officer is the kind of thing I can actually get you some jail time for, and"—he put his face close to hers until they were nose to nose—"I'm really going to en-joy it."

With that, Hugh Cramer turned and walked away. Even his stride was smug, Kendra noted.

She might have messed up this one, she admitted to herself. But for once she was completely in the right.

She trudged from the courthouse and down the steps.

There waited Vickie Sawyer from Channel Seven news. *This just keeps getting better.*

"Miss Simms, it seems we meet again."

Kendra smirked. "I'd probably miss you if you ever left me alone, Miss Sawyer." Vickie Sawyer followed Kendra every time she had any kind of problem with the law. She had become Vickie's showpiece, as it were.

"Should I turn the camera on now, or wait until after you insult me?" Sawyer retorted.

"Oh, by all means, why would I want all of Fort White to miss seeing you insulted?"

The other woman motioned to her camera-man, who remained poised behind her. The mechanical hum and red light on his equipment let Kendra know she was now being recorded.

"I'm standing with Kendra Simms of the Seaton Animal Rescue team to discuss her latest court hearing. Is it true that you assaulted a police officer, Miss Simms?"

"No, it is not. Now, if you will excuse me, I have better people to be antagonized by." She slung her canvas bag onto one shoulder and took a few steps.

Vickie's voice behind her was loud and clear. "Do you think the Rescue will ask for your resignation with your latest legal problem?"

Kendra made an about-face. "What did you say?"

"A board member contacted this morning for comment told Channel Seven news that your contract is up this year, and the negative publicity you generated isn't good for the Seaton Animal Rescue." A self-satisfied expression crossed Vickie's pretty features.

Keep your cool, Kendra told herself. "I believe that the board of directors of the Rescue are some of the best people in this county and will take care of its business in a professional manner."

"What if that professionalism means your resignation?"

Vickie had her, and they both knew it. "I'll do whatever is deemed best for the Rescue, of course. Now, if you'll excuse me, I have a defense to plan."

"*You* have a defense to plan?" Vickie's eyes flashed brightly at the possibility of something new to report. "Why isn't your attorney doing that?"

"I'm going to defend myself. Now, as I said, I need to leave."

Could a board member really have told Vickie that she would be fired over this? Kendra made her way to her car, mentally reviewing the list of board members. Could someone she trusted have said that?

"I heard your interview."

The voice from behind her took her off guard, and she dropped her keys.

Hugh Cramer leaned over and picked them up. Holding them out to her, he said, "I don't believe the Rescue will fire you. If they were going to, they'd probably have done it the time we got you for stealing those cats."

"The woman was starving those cats, and"—she held up a finger for emphasis— "she had stolen each and every one of them herself." She grabbed the keys from his hand. "What do you want, Mr. Cramer?"

"A plea bargain."

"Not on your life. I didn't do anything to that man, and he knows it."

Mr. Cramer put his briefcase down on the

ground and took her keys from her. As he spoke, he unlocked her car door. "This man—the officer—has a pretty good track record. I'd hate to see either of you hurt your reputations in court."

She watched the news van pulling away from the curb. "I appreciate your concern, but it seems like I'm already ruined. Anyway, I thought you wanted me to go to jail."

"Yeah, well, I've thought about it."

When their eyes met, the gentleness in his gaze made her relax a bit.

"Is the cop really serious about this?"

"That's why I waited here. I just got off my cell with the chief of police. I believe he *is* serious. Maybe you should tell me what really happened."

She stiffened. "I already told you what happened. If that isn't good enough, I'll see you in court." She paused and studied him. "By the way, you can't talk about my past during the trial, can you?

"No, I—"

A smile tugged at her lips. "That information made my day. If you'll excuse me, I'm going home to write my opening statement."

"Of course . . ." He spoke as if thinking aloud. ". . . since I *can* prove that this is a *pattern* of behavior . . . yeah, as a matter of fact, I probably can bring up your past legal problems."

Kendra stared at him in disbelief.

"Think about it, though," he continued. "Even if I do, it's not as if most of the county doesn't already know your record."

"I could ask Judge Cole to let me be tried in another county, though, couldn't I?"

"I don't see that happening, Miss Simms. You'd have a lot to prove to get him to agree to a change of venue. Truth is, you need an attorney. Go get one, unless you want to end up in deep trouble."

"I'm not already in deep trouble?"

"Well, let's say deeper trouble, then."

Frustrated, she got into her SUV and drove off, watching Cramer in her rearview mirror watching her until she was out of sight.

Kendra changed her strategy.

With turnip in hand, she headed out to the wooded area where all her problems had begun. She would track down that pig, and she would find it a home.

"Here, piggy." Her voice was barely above a whisper. "Here, piggy, piggy, piggy." She walked softly, trying not to make noise. Carrying a medium-sized dog crate, she wondered how in the world she'd carry it back after adding ten to fifteen pounds of potbellied pig.

Something rustled. She put the carrier down and placed the turnip in it. Then she purposefully moved away from the wire crate, hoping the little ham would march in after the turnip.

He didn't let her down. As soon as she cleared the crate's entrance, the pig stormed it. She slammed the cage door shut when she saw it was safely inside.

She danced a little jig of accomplishment but wasn't prepared for what happened next. She'd thought the animal would just sit down with its supper and munch. But piggy had different ideas. With everything in it, it tried to escape. It rammed the door until it bent. It squealed and bit the wires; it did everything Kendra didn't expect and more.

It took almost an hour before it calmed down. She shook her head, afraid for the little thing's health; no animal could be that upset and not have a rise in blood pressure.

Talking to it in a low, soothing tone, she took a step toward the carrier. The potbelly watched her with the eyes of a predator. *When had pigs become so aggressive?* She picked up the cage and did her best to carry it to the house. Several times she had to put it down until the animal calmed down again. After which she'd heave-ho and walk another few steps until the pig got upset again or became too heavy to carry.

When she finally reached her driveway, she wedged the wire crate into the back of her SUV and hoped the animal would be all right long enough to get to the Rescue. Then she realized that she needed a vet who knew about pigs. She made a quick call on her cell.

When she turned toward her house, what she found was her worst enemy, Hugh Cramer, camped on her doorstep.

She slammed the hatchback door closed. "What are you doing here?" she demanded.

Inside the car, the pig went wild.

With a furrowed brow, Cramer asked, "What in the name of all that's holy do you have in there?"

She strode up to where he sat, got into his face, and spoke very ominously. "Something that will eat you if you don't leave me alone."

Hugh Cramer rubbed a hand through his short brown hair. "I thought we'd made friends back there outside the courthouse."

"Then you read way too much into it. You still want to prosecute me, right?"

He shrugged. "Not really."

Excitement coursed through her veins. "No? Really? Then it's all over?"

His grin might have been infectious, had the ogre of the woods not been pitching a tantrum in the carrier in her car. "*You* read way too much into *that*. I said I didn't *want* to prosecute you. But the law is the law, you know. In fact, before you let that monster out of your car, why don't you tell me exactly what happened. I may be able to help you."

"The word *satan* comes from a root meaning *adversary* or *accuser*. Did you know that?" She banged a fist against the car. "Will you calm down in there, please?"

The snorting and squealing suddenly stopped.

In surprise, she swiveled back around to her prisoner, wondering what had happened in the little holding cell.

Cramer moved to the hatchback and opened it. "You have a potbellied pig in here." Amazement filled his eyes. "There can't be two of them in all of Fort White. This just can't be."

She nodded. "I think someone dropped him off in the woods behind our house."

"When you said the fight was about a pig, I pictured a full-size sow. Not this little thing. That's what this is about?"

She hesitated. "As I said at the courthouse, this is all a misunderstanding."

Cramer reached for the carrier's handle, but

the pig went on the attack. He drew back quickly. "What's its problem?"

"I'm not sure. I don't know enough about pigs to tell you. I need a vet with a farm-animal background to examine him."

The pig continued its tirade.

Cramer's eyes filled with compassion. "My best friends have one of those as a pet. Do you think this one went wild, and that's why its owners dropped it off here?"

"All I know is that my neighbor, Len Hicks, wanted pork chops."

"Hicks wanted to eat it? That's incredible." He faked a shudder. "That'd be like eating a puppy." He reached toward the cage again and again averted the pig's move to nip him. "Do you need help getting it somewhere?"

"No, I have a couple of volunteers due here in a few minutes." She paused. "The critter *is* awfully wild." She hated to admit it.

"Well, wild or not, that's no reason to arrest you. If your neighbor wanted dinner, there's always fast food. Let me see what I can do."

His grin disarmed her. "Do you mean that?"

"I don't want this case any more than you do. For goodness' sake, you're already a mar-tyr for animal rights around here. It doesn't help me that I'll have to prosecute you for the umpteenth time."

She held up three fingers. "Third, but who's counting?"

"Oh, that's right. And as I recall, you were held in contempt by Judge Delaney that last time. Almost spent the night in jail, right?"

"I made a public apology," she argued.

"What was the fine again?"

"From *my* budget? Lots. Just leave it at that."

"Don't ever ask a judge if she scares little children for kicks again, okay?" He winked. "Just a bit of free legal advice."

She thought for a moment, then said what was on her mind. "Do you keep pulling my cases because Walter Henry thinks you want his job, and he knows prosecuting me makes you look bad?"

He studied her with steel blue eyes. "Where did you hear that?"

She shrugged. "That's the story from your office."

He seemed to say more to himself than to her, "Does everyone think this but me?"

"Apparently so. I asked around about you, and people told me that if you could get some big cases under your belt, you'd make a great DA."

"That's not what I want. I just want to put bad guys behind bars." He took a long breath and studied the ground. When his gaze returned to hers, the gentleness she'd seen earlier was back. "I'll make some calls. Talk to you in a few days."

As he walked to his car, she called after him, "Hugh?"

He spun around, his smile making her pulse slightly erratic. "Are we on a first-name basis now?" he asked.

She found it impossible not to return the smile and move toward him. "I think so." She touched his hand, not expecting to feel a bolt of lightning course through her. "Thank you." Her words were but a whisper.

He pulled his hand away. Did he feel it too? He must have, because his tone sounded a little . . . different. "Don't mention it. And I mean that. Oh, and stay off TV in the future— at least on this, okay?"

No problem on her part. She hated facing Miss Channel Seven. "Sure." She liked his smile; it somehow reassured her.

"I'll be calling you."

"I'll be waiting."

As he headed for his car, a van pulled into her driveway, and two men exited it. One of them took a gander at Hugh and asked, "Aren't you the guy trying to put Kendra in jail?"

"That's not how I'd put it." Hugh opened his car door as he spoke.

"Well, that's your story. You don't need to be here bothering her. She has work to do, and you're a nuisance."

Kendra listened to the exchange and remarked to Hugh, "Remember when you said the law was the law?" Written all over her face was *I told you so.* "It's called freedom of speech."

"Yeah, yeah. I'll get on that matter and see what I can do." He left with a curt nod to the volunteers.

Chapter Two

"Kendra dear, pass me the pot, and for goodness' sake cool down."

Kendra handed her mother a small clay pot and watched Vera Simms plant seedlings. "You don't understand. This time I'm in real trouble."

"Poppycock! You're not in trouble. You just think you are. You always manage to find a way out of these things." She put the pot aside and took off her gardening gloves. The small patio on which they stood heated under the noon sun. "Would you like a drink, dear?"

"Sure." Kendra shrugged, wishing her mother would take her predicament seriously.

"You'll see, sweetie. You'll be as right as

25

rain after some sweet iced tea and a good break." Vera walked through the back door of their home and immediately began to scream to Kendra, "Hurry, dear! Hurry!"

The small television on the kitchen counter was giving the noon news. Kendra's interview didn't play well. She came across as a snob, probably because she'd been put on the spot by Vickie Sawyer and was trying to avoid answering her questions.

What she didn't expect was to see a tape of herself on a talk show from last year. The local show host had asked her, "What would you do to save an animal?"

"That's not the question," she'd replied. "The question is, what *wouldn't* I do? The answer is, there is nothing I wouldn't do to protect a creature that can't protect itself."

Vickie Sawyer's image then replaced Kendra's own. "And that's it. There's no doubt that this woman has become so caught up in her cause, she's forgotten about the laws of the land. Just for the record, this is her third offense. Back to you, Sam."

The anchor took over the show as Kendra sat at the kitchen table. "I can't believe she's coming after me like this."

Her mother didn't speak; she prepared their tea and sat opposite her.

"What should I do?" Kendra buried her face in her hands.

Her mother sighed. "Find a good attorney. This isn't something you should play around with."

Kendra glanced at her mom. "Your tune has sure changed."

Her mother pursed her lips. "I spoke before I saw how the media is handling the situation."

Kendra sipped her tea. "I can't afford a lawyer."

"I'll help you."

Kendra waved away the offer. "I'm not taking money from you."

The older woman's hurt was obvious. Kendra reached out and touched her hand. "I appreciate it, though."

"What's your next move?"

"I'm going to have to play some media games myself."

"I'm so glad you live here. You're so much fun. Nothing like your sister, who's wonderful, but in a different way. Of course, your father would roll over in his grave if he knew about your civil disobedience."

Kendra sipped her tea, thoughts of protest marches and provocative sound bites going through her mind.

Nonchalantly the older woman asked, "Dear, are you going out tonight?"

"I thought I'd run over to the Rescue and check on the pig."

Her mother acted coy. "If you don't mind, would you use the outside stairway this evening?"

"You have a date!" Kendra's words came out as an accusation.

Her mother looked irritated. "I believe you're crossing the mother-daughter line, dear. If I had a date, it wouldn't be any of your business. I've been single for many years."

"I believe we crossed that line a long time ago, *dear.* So who is he? Where'd you meet him?"

"We met at a flower show, and his name is not your concern. Now go see your pig."

For a moment they just stared at each other.

Finally Kendra said, "No matter how you say it, 'go see your pig' just doesn't sound right."

Vera nodded her agreement.

Including some horrible construction traffic, the shelter was only about twenty minutes away. Kendra hummed softly along with the radio as she turned the corner into the development where the Rescue was located. The house closest to the entrance of the shelter had a SOLD sign in the front yard and a police car parked in the drive. As she drove by she noticed the word CHIEF on the back of the vehicle.

The developer had done a beautiful job with this project, she mused. The homes ranged from Tudor to ranch, each one more beautiful than the next. She could readily understand how a person of Chief Marvin Cary's stature in the community would want to live there.

She used her remote to unlock the shelter's gate and enter the property. After parking, she went in to check on the little brat.

A volunteer, who was also a computer whiz, jumped from her seat upon Kendra's arrival. "You won't believe this! I found a man in Wisconsin with proper references to take Old Brown Dog."

"No kidding! A vet approved him, along with his local shelter?"

Joan's grin stretched from ear to ear. "Yep! I can't believe we found a home for the old fella. The man's going to drive down next week to get him. Isn't that the best news you've heard all day?"

"It is. I don't know how you got into this network of animal lovers, Joan, but you're the main reason we can be a no-kill shelter." She hugged the younger woman. "Thank you."

When Joan pulled away from Kendra, she went back to her computer. "I enjoy it. It's a way I can help, even though most people see me as a geek."

"Just because you're eighteen and not dating doesn't make you a geek."

Joan rolled her eyes. "I don't even have a decent job."

Kendra reached down and patted the top of Joan's head. "You have a job. It's a job that always pays on time, and the checks don't bounce. That's worth something."

Grabbing her purse, Joan didn't appear convinced of her worth. "I'm a cashier at a supermarket."

"That's a great way to put yourself through college. You're asking way too much of yourself way too soon."

"But think of all you do, Kendra. You stand up for animals's rights, you protest their mistreatment—you do all kinds of wonderful things."

"I hadn't done them at eighteen. You need to remember, I'll hit thirty this year. Also, I have wonderful volunteers—like you—who help find the pets homes."

Joan shrugged, then checked her watch. "I

gotta go. My mom asked me to be home for supper, since I'm not working this evening."

"That's nice, Joanie. Go home, eat with your parents, and have a good evening. And remember, without you, the pets might stay here forever."

After Joan left, Kendra headed to the kennel area. She spoke softly to all the animals, mainly dogs and cats, and gave them treats. Old Brown Dog wagged his tail and accepted his biscuit with what appeared to be a smile. Kendra thought about his new owner. What a lucky person. This old critter would give love unconditionally and ask nothing in return but a snack and a pat on the head.

She tried to give each animal a little attention. It wasn't easy, as they had sixteen dogs and ten cats in the shelter at the moment.

They also had one little piggy.

Kendra stretched out beside the cage that held her newest find. In her already dirty jeans and T-shirt, she rolled over onto her back and asked the pig, "Are you ever going to calm down? Just a little—that's all I ask."

The pig squealed and once again rammed the door, and Kendra worried about how much longer she could keep the pig if it didn't settle in better.

Words from the veterinarian didn't help

either. She'd agreed that the pig had probably been someone's pet but had either gotten loose or been turned out. And pigs, she'd said, could go wild, or feral, in as little as three weeks.

But maybe she could find the owners and return the little guy—oops, *gal,* she'd learned— and the pig would be someone else's problem.

Unfortunately, she'd also learned that pigs were higher-strung than almost any other animal. This girl could actually give herself a heart attack if she didn't compose herself.

The vet had given Kendra something to calm her new friend—if only she could get her to eat it—and said she'd be back to check on her.

She pulled herself from the floor and dusted herself off. When the doors opened to the kennel area, she expected the vet, but Hugh Cramer walked through them, dressed in jeans and a polo shirt. Whether he was her enemy or not, she couldn't help the tugging she felt at her lips. She hadn't realized how muscular the guy was. She'd only ever seen him in a suit.

"So, how's our little buddy?"

The pig squealed and bit the wire door of her cage.

Kendra smiled halfheartedly. "I have to go get something from the kitchen. If you'll wait here, I'll fill you in."

Upon her return she found Hugh trying to calm the pig with gentle murmurs. He met her eyes with a sheepish grin. "I don't normally talk to animals."

"So you don't think you're Dr. Dolittle, then?"

"Hardly."

She spoke with cool authority. "I found out some things I didn't know."

While pouring the oozy liquid the vet had given her onto a carrot, Kendra informed him of what the vet had said. Checking her watch, she told Hugh she was expecting the vet to return shortly.

"So, the little buddy is a buddette, huh?" Hugh watched the pig through the cage.

Even though he seemed jovial, Kendra sensed something in his mood that wasn't.

"Looks just like Joey," he said.

"You know a pig named Joey?" Kendra paused. "Did I really just say that?"

He chuckled. "I know a pig, yes. I told you, my best friends own one. Danni and Michael Sommars."

Kendra bent over and pushed the carrot through the cage, dropping it within reach of the pig. "Sommars? Why do I know that name?" She pulled herself to full height.

"Big lawsuit some years back."

"Oh, right. My very first arrest! I was in the crowd that picketed at Fairmont Farms over the pig's treatment."

"I know I'm going to hate myself for asking, but why were you arrested that time?"

When she stole a glance at him, she again noticed how well he filled out his clothing. Maybe this office guy worked out. His arms were certainly muscular.

"Um . . ." For a moment she'd forgotten his question. "Oh, well, you know how it is."

His face split into a devilish, handsome grin, white teeth against his tanned face. "No. Not really." He folded his arms over his expansive chest. "Go ahead and explain. I'm listening."

"Well . . ." She stumbled through her speech, reflecting sadly that his usual business suit hid all his good qualities. "The Fairmonts were not being nice to Joey. They just wanted him because potbellies were trendy, and they thought they could make money off him. They dressed him up and paraded him about mercilessly as their mascot. So about twenty of us got together and protested at their place, waving signs and yelling things like, 'Joey is more than just money.' Of course, we used the dollar sign instead of the word. . . ." Her voice trailed off.

"You used the dollar sign when you yelled?"

"No!" She got flustered, and instead of being able to rebut him, she just wanted to stare into his azure eyes. "When we painted it on the signs, we used the symbol."

"Ah, the memories. When you painted signs and yelled at farms. So you were arrested for trespassing and illegal congress, huh?"

"Yeah. But it worked. And Michael Sommars adopted Joey. I bet he's good to him too."

"They treat him like he's their child." His expression became more solemn. "I have something to tell you."

Kendra's eyes were downcast. "I know. I could almost see it in your face."

He hesitated. "We're adding charges of disobeying a direct command from a police officer and resisting arrest."

She drew a deep breath and let it out slowly. "Are you kidding me? Can you tell me who's behind this farce?"

"I can only say that when you are tried, it will put you in a bad light and my career in the toilet. You should find representation."

Sounding much more confident than she felt, she said perkily, "O ye of little faith. I can defend myself—I was the president of my college debate team."

"Why does that not surprise me?"

With each lost in their own thoughts, a silence fell over the pair.

Finally she asked, "What else should I do?"

He bent down to the pig's cage. "First you need to get your little hamlet domesticated, or you'll never get her adopted."

"I wasn't talking about her."

He rose. She didn't move away, even realizing she could smell his cologne and feel the warmth he exuded.

His voice resonated through her like warm cider on a cold winter's night. "I can't help you further and still be ethical."

"But can't you get the charges dropped?"

"If I could, I wouldn't be here."

The tension of the moment took Kendra's breath away. Unless she was mistaken, he felt it as well, the lightning crackling through the room like a sudden heat wave. How had they come to this?

She nodded as he turned and walked away.

It hurt to watch him leave, but that was the way it had to be.

At least for now.

Kendra found herself in the kennel area again the next morning, wondering how she'd get the little gal used to her cage.

"Hello?"

Another voice in the room startled Kendra. "May I help you?" she asked.

A lovely woman with black hair and warm brown eyes stood in the doorway. "If you're Kendra Simms, I want to introduce myself and find out if I can help you with your new pet."

"Hamlette is my problem, not my pet."

The woman laughed. "I understand *that* if anyone does. I'm Danni Sommars."

The pig started its usual rampage.

Kendra just shook her head at the sound. "Hugh Cramer sent you, didn't he?"

"He did. He called and asked me to stop by to see if I could answer any questions for you. About potbellies."

Kendra crossed her arms. "I'll bet he mentioned that I need a lawyer as well."

Danni Sommars looked surprised. "No. But if it's criminal, I don't do criminal law anyway."

"I see." Kendra lowered her guard. "Hamlette is wild."

Danni would have had to be blind and deaf not to already know this, what with the noise the pig made. She continued watching the animal, her face a study in contemplation. "Tell you what I'll do. My Joey is domesticated. I read somewhere that putting a settled animal with one that's wild can do some good. But let me set a few ground rules."

"Rules?"

Danni continued. "Joey is part of my family, just like my kids and my dog. You'll need to get Hamlette, as you call her, into one of the bigger cages." She pointed at the larger ones. "You should give her a few days to get used to that. Then we'll bring Joey by, and you'll leave him outside her cage so he won't get hurt."

"I appreciate your help, but I can't leave an animal outside the cages. I can put him in the one next to hers."

Danni eyed the cages again and then looked at Kendra. "That might work. But if I see that Joey gets upset, he comes right home."

"That's fair enough."

"Isn't it funny?" Danni shook her head. "Hugh reminded me that your protests at Fairmont Farms are what led to my meeting my husband and our adopting Joey. Now Joey can help you out."

"I'm glad he ended up in a nice home, Danni."

"Why don't you come to dinner tomorrow night and meet him and the rest of my family? This might work better if Joey gets to know you first."

Surprised by the offer, Kendra agreed. "That's great. Thank you."

The phone rang as Danni wrote down her address and phone number for Kendra. She allowed the machine to pick it up, but once Danni was gone, Kendra got the message and returned the call.

"Miss Simms, this is Josephine Wellington of the Clinton Heights Community Organization. I need to speak with you regarding the animal sanctuary you run. I appreciate your calling me back. Could you meet with us tomorrow night?"

Kendra didn't like something about the invitation, though she couldn't say why. "I'd be glad to. But what is it you need me for?"

"Since the sanctuary is practically in our backyard, we'd like to hear more about it, that's all."

"I'd love to come, then. Thank you." After finding out the time and address, Kendra hung up.

Talking about the Rescue to community groups was one of her favorite parts of the job. This could be even better, since the Clinton Heights development was obviously a high end one, with residents who would have lots of money to donate.

Maybe this wasn't turning out to be such a bad week after all.

Dressed in a long pencil skirt, sandals, and a belted blouse, Kendra twirled in front of her mirror. She hoped her attire would be right for this meeting. The people there were out of her social circle; in fact, they were the "society" of the city.

As she got into her car and started it, she reviewed what she might need. In her briefcase were brochures, statistics, anything anyone could possibly want to know about the Rescue. She prepared herself for all questions.

But the real reason she'd been summoned to Clinton Heights became clear soon after she parked her car.

As she approached the clubhouse, she noticed Hugh Cramer talking to a tall man with blond hair. Even from the back she knew it was Chief of Police Marvin Cary.

Although it was a warm spring evening, Kendra felt chilled.

When Hugh saw her, surprise registered on his handsome face.

"So good to meet you, Kendra." An older woman pulled Kendra into the club house.

"I'm Mrs. Wellington. I'm the one who called you last evening. I hope you're well?"

A gleam in the woman's eye told Kendra that whatever lay ahead would not be favorable to her. She pretended not to notice the patronizing tone of Mrs. Wellington's voice. "I'm quite well and ready to answer any questions you might have about the Seaton Animal Rescue."

"Please get yourself some punch and cake to celebrate our first official meeting."

Just as the woman suggested that, Kendra saw several cameramen come through the door. All three of the local stations were represented, and she recognized Lew Johnson from the biggest newspaper in town.

Ambushed.

The adrenaline pumped through her veins as she saw the press setting up in the back of the room.

Mrs. Wellington watched her, and she glared at the woman, speaking in a perfectly calm manner. "You will rue the day you tried to play *my* game." She handed off her briefcase and purse to the woman. "Here, hold these. I have some old friends to greet."

She doubted that anyone at the meeting expected her to walk up to one of the TV station managers, Pete Randall, and actually hug him. "How are you?"

His voice held warm affection. "Still waiting for you, sweetie. When do I get my chance?"

"When we're the same age."

"I started counting backward ten years ago, so I only have ten more years to go. Why not put me out of my agony?"

She whispered, "Why not tell me why you're here?"

The man's face fell. The bright smile he'd had for her a moment ago vanished. "You weren't told?"

"I thought I was here to tell the Clinton Heights Community Organization about the Seaton Animal Rescue."

He took a glance around the room. "We've got to find out who set you up. We are here to get the lowdown on your court case. I see the ADA Cramer. You think it's him?"

She caught Hugh in her sights. "I don't *want* to think so."

"He doesn't seem the type to me either. Hey, do I get a scoop on your assault on a police officer?"

"If you ask a lot of questions tonight and make me look beautiful on the eleven o'clock news."

"Sounds good. I'll get some sound bites to

show everyone the princess you are." He kissed her cheek right there in front of the world.

Hugh didn't like it. Who'd this guy think he was? This whole thing had turned out to be a setup, and one of the snipers kissed her? He didn't like it one bit.

"Are you ready?" The chief of police's question jarred Hugh from his reverie.

"Ready? Ready for what?"

"We thought you could clarify why the Seaton Animal Rescue, which is in our backyard, has an accused criminal in charge."

A moment ago Hugh was angry. Then, after seeing the kiss, he was furious. Now he was almost beyond control. "You set me up for this, didn't you? You could have told me what you wanted. But instead you asked me to speak on the rate of crimes in the county." He turned to leave.

"You wouldn't have come otherwise, Cramer," Cary called from behind him. "We all know you go easy on Kendra Simms."

Hugh spun back to the man. "You son of a—" He stopped in midsentence and took a deep breath. "Have you forgotten that my commenting on an ongoing investigation is against the law?"

"Like we always say at the precinct, 'We get 'em, and the lawyers set 'em free.' "

"What would you have me do?" Hugh asked brusquely. "Break the law for you?"

"I'd have you work for the good of the county and not for your own political ambitions. I don't think a lawyer can do that, though." Cary walked away.

Hugh angrily decided to stay put and play the lousy hand he'd been dealt as well as he could. As he took a seat near the front of the room, Cary asked everyone for their attention. He proceeded to tell the attendees about the debate he would be having with Miss Simms regarding the Seaton Animal Rescue and her arrest.

Hugh figured Kendra was another pawn in the chief's game.

After taking a seat behind the table at the front of the room, Kendra asked, "Now, where did my secretary go?"

Mrs. Wellington, whom Hugh knew from various charity functions, brought Kendra her briefcase. The expression on her face let the whole place know she wasn't anyone's secretary.

"Thank you so much for keeping my things safe for me. Everyone, let's give Josephine Wellington a hand." Kendra led the faint applause.

Clapping loudly, Pete Randall laughed, then made it sound like a cough.

Hugh choked back the same response. He'd seen Kendra when her back was against the wall. Cary and his friends were in for a little surprise.

"It was my understanding that the people of Clinton Heights wanted information on the Seaton Animal Rescue. I have brochures for everyone. There's enough for the media too. Of course, they probably already have them memorized." Her smile caught Hugh off guard. Even under fire this woman could pull off a manner of complete confidence. "The shelter has been here for over five years. I took over the role of administrator several years ago, after being a volunteer since its opening."

She gave the audience all the statistics on the Rescue. She explained that they were a no-kill shelter and that they found homes for dogs and cats all over the country. When asked about her legal case, she said simply, "If you want that information, you have to hear the important facts first."

Pete Randall asked most of the questions, which kept the Rescue in a good light.

That is, until Marvin Cary got to his feet and said, "Enough of this drivel. We want to know about the charges pending against you. The Assistant DA is here. Let him tell us."

Hugh got up and faced Kendra as he buttoned his jacket. "I can't legally comment on an ongoing investigation. I will say that all the facts are not in, and every accused person is innocent until proven otherwise."

If looks could kill, Cary would have been guilty of murder.

Kendra's mouth curved into a smile after Hugh's short speech. "I would be glad to answer whatever questions I can."

"Did you assault Officer Bert Gibson?" asked one reporter.

"No. I didn't. He was on the scene when I was chasing a stray animal, and he got knocked over."

Vickie Sawyer jumped into the fray. "The police report states that you maliciously stabbed him."

"I had a carrot in my hand. If an officer serving this community is afraid of a carrot, we need to rethink what type of training our police cadets go through."

Another hand went up as the meeting became a news conference. "What about the other man? Did he or did he not have a gun?"

"He did. He stated he was going to kill the small potbellied pig and eat it."

A collective gasp came from her audience. Obviously the group lacked the hunting spirit.

"Since this city knows all about the fight several years ago for the Fairmont Farms mascot, you can see why I tried to protect the little thing."

"But," Vickie Sawyer shouted, "you assaulted a policeman in your eagerness to help a pig."

Kendra stood up and walked around the table. All the cameras turned to her. "I stand five-foot-three. If I can beat up a cop, we need new cops. How can they protect your families if someone of my stature can kick their butts?

"This is the bottom line, folks. I didn't do anything wrong. It's become transparent that someone with political pull"—she nodded toward the police chief—"wants this ridiculous case tried. So you have to ask yourself, now that you have the particulars, is prosecuting me the right thing to do? Call your county commissioners, and let them know what you think.

"I certainly appreciate Mrs. Wellington's invitation. And I hope you all have a wonderful evening." Kendra grabbed her purse and briefcase and left before anyone said anything else.

The murmurings from the Clinton Heights

residents ranged from "She's right, this is stupid" to "I think I'll call my commissioner on her behalf."

The ambush had backfired, thank God, Hugh reflected. Maybe now he could get back to prosecuting real cases.

Chapter Three

"I walked into an ambush." Kendra sipped her cola. "There I was in the clubhouse, ready to give my spiel about the Rescue, and I find out I'm under attack instead."

"Do you know who called the press?" Danni Sommars had the "lawyer" look in her eyes. Although the evening was a pleasant one, Kendra could see her new friend's legal mind at work.

"From what Pete Randall said, it was Cary's office that called him."

Danni raised her glass. "To good old Pete, who's made my life miserable on more than one occasion."

Kendra raised her glass. "I'm sorry, but he likes me."

"Don't worry about it. In your position you need all the friendly press you can get."

Danni checked her watch. "My husband should be home with the kids any minute now. I'll put the lasagna in the oven then. Is it getting too late for you? Do you have to be anywhere?"

"No. This is great. I haven't let my hair down in what feels like forever."

A grunt at her feet reminded her of another new friend. Joey lay sleeping near her in the den of the Sommars' home.

"If only Hamlette would behave like this."

"I'm just glad Joey took to you the way he did. Now I can let you use him with her."

"I put her in the big cage like you told me to. I think that alone helped. She doesn't bite the wires now."

"Anyone home?" Hugh Cramer walked into the den in jeans and a T-shirt. "Kendra?" he said in obvious surprise.

"Hugh, what are you doing here?"

"I invited him tonight as well." Danni's gaze darted between their shocked faces. "Is that a problem?"

Hugh explained the situation. "Danni, I'm prosecuting Kendra."

"How was I supposed to know that?"

Kendra spoke up. "Maybe from the paper?"

"Wait a minute!" Danni rose and moved toward Hugh. "You're prosecuting Kendra, and you're helping her too? Hugh! What are you trying to do to your career? I can't believe you'd do this." She focused on Kendra. "No offense intended, but he's about to commit occupational suicide."

"I know!" Hugh belted out. "I didn't know you'd invited Kendra. I can leave."

Kendra wouldn't hear of it. "No, I'll go. Thanks for everything, Danni."

"That's my call. Hugh will leave." Danni looked at him with accusing eyes. "We *will* talk tomorrow."

In a slightly sarcastic tone he told her, "Can't wait." He walked toward the door and gazed back at Kendra. "Good show last night." With that, he left.

"Okay, tell me what's going on. Surely I can do something." Danni sat down and motioned for Kendra to do the same.

Kendra obeyed but hesitantly. "I didn't mean to ruin your evening, Danni."

"To be honest, I am worried about Hugh. He's a good guy, you know. So start at the beginning."

Kendra did, leaving out only how Hugh made her feel slightly breathless at times.

Danni studied Kendra, then quirked a questioning brow. "Did you tell me the part where you like him, or did I miss that?"

Kendra couldn't hide her shock. "He's a very nice guy."

"No, no. This isn't just anyone you're talking to. This is a really special situation. I've been there. You're falling for him, aren't you?"

Kendra's cheeks filled with heat.

"Oh, my! You are! This is so exciting and so wrong all at the same time."

Kendra took a long drink of her cola and waited for Danni to say something else. Before she could, however, Danni's husband entered with their children.

"Hey, sweetie." He kissed Danni and handed her a bundle of little girl.

Danni took the child and made introductions. "Kendra, my husband, Michael. Our kids, Cole and Leanne."

Cole darted to where Kendra sat and plopped down next to Joey, who was still snoring softly at her feet.

"How old are you?" Kendra asked the boy.

"I'm three. Leanne is only one, so she's still a baby, but I'm a big boy." He sat happily petting the pig that stretched after being awakened.

"Come with me, Kendra." Danni still held

the toddler. "We need to talk and to get some more ice for our drinks. I'll put dinner in, and we'll make a salad."

"What about Hugh?"

Danni motioned for Kendra to follow her to the kitchen. "What did you think we were going to talk about?"

Hamlette went out of her mind upon seeing another pig. She squealed, rammed the cage, and even tried to climb the sides.

Joey, however, took it all in stride. He made soft noises in his cage next to hers and lay down beyond where she could try to nip him.

"Amazing." Kendra found it hard to believe that a pig could be so poised.

Danni did not. "He's used to dealing with tension, at least in people. He works in the pet therapy program in Trentville. My brother, Alex Price, has a clinic where they offer it. Joey's reputation has me getting e-mail from all over the country from places that want to use him."

"How do you say no?"

"I leave that up to my sister-in-law, Beth. She uses a form letter to explain that Joey doesn't leave this area, and she refers them to a national registry that's truly remarkable."

They watched as Joey moved a little closer

to Hamlette and lay back down. The other pig calmed down but kept an eye on him.

"What does your sister-in-law do for a living?"

"She's the clinic administrator. And she keeps a listing of pets used for patient therapy and where they're located. Usually she can find an animal within driving distance of whoever's requested one."

"That's unique."

"That's my family. Animal lovers all. Some call us odd. I prefer unique."

Hamlette squealed and rammed the cage on Joey's side. Joey backed up and lay down again.

Both women started at the noise.

Danni didn't take her eyes off her pet. "Move him from this cage into one not directly next to hers if you're not here."

She picked up her purse to leave. "And, Kendra, make sure you call an attorney about your case. I can give you a list a mile long, or, in this one case, maybe Michael or I can even do it."

"Honestly, I don't have a lot of money."

"Hey, what are friends for?"

In his office, Hugh couldn't get Kendra out of his mind. She'd looked like a million dollars in jeans. Not all women, at least in his opinion, could really carry off jeans.

But Kendra Simms could.

And well.

He needed to stay away from her, though. She could melt a man with one touch. He rubbed his right hand, remembering how her electricity had jolted him.

"Get over it," he told himself as he picked up the messages Lydia had left for him.

Unfortunately, one of the calls was from his mother. She had her sights set on his dating a woman she'd introduced him to. The woman definitely had things going for her, including great looks. However, there was more to life than that, and Hugh couldn't stomach her whiny, get-her-own-way attitude. Celia Blake. There was a name to forget. Or, if remembered, to hide from.

Impressed that Judge Cole had called, he returned that summons first.

When the judge came on the line, he said, "Hugh?"

"Yes, sir."

"This is Thomas Cole. We need to talk about this Kendra Simms situation."

"Why is that, sir?"

"She's . . . *Feisty* would be a good word for her. But she probably didn't really hurt anyone.

I'm ready to retire, and I really don't want this one on my record."

"I couldn't agree more. I thought I'd go see the witness and the police officer."

"Good. That's what I hoped you'd say. Now, on to more pleasant things. You remember the Fourth of July party we're having?"

"I'll be there."

"You'd better be. I'm retiring with that party, and I want *all* my kids there."

"I wouldn't miss it."

The judge's voice became a little gruff, and he cleared his throat. "Well, see to it you don't." He hung up.

Hugh sat there for a moment and thought about the judge. He was a good man, one Hugh admired more than mere words could say. If Hugh had a hero, it would be Thomas Cole.

As for his own thoughts on the Kendra Simms case, they were exactly the same as the judge's. Neither of them wanted to be remembered for this prosecution. The arraignment had been fun, but the time of truth had come, and Hugh would not blow it.

For everyone's sake, he'd better not.

He had started out attempting to find out exactly what had happened the day Kendra caught her pig, but he'd ended up in a hostile situation. He'd gotten Bert Gibson, the police officer in Kendra's case, and Len Hicks, the "witness"—and he used that term loosely— together to go over their testimony.

What a joke.

These men needed a life and had evidently decided that being bested by a woman chasing a pig was the way to get their fifteen minutes of fame.

Gibson had a record as a reliable kind of guy. In fact, the words *reliable, honest,* and *decent* came up often in his personnel file. And no one had told Hugh anything different.

Then there was Len Hicks. He thought the whole case a rocking good time. Hugh watched them together and knew he didn't have a snowball's chance in the netherworld of winning this case.

After they'd done all their talking, making the story a little more colorful with each telling, Hugh ran a hand through his hair.

Then something Hugh hadn't expected happened. The chief of police, Marvin Cary, was ushered in by Hugh's secretary.

Hugh stood as he entered, but the man waved him back to his seat.

"Have we got her yet?" Cary acted like a happy man.

"Got whom, sir?" Hugh asked.

"That damn Simms girl! She gets away with too much in this town, and I'm going to like watching her go down. I want her this time, Mr. Cramer. Do not plead her out to anything less than jail time."

For Cary's benefit, so the chief could see how ridiculous this prosecution would be, Hugh turned his attention back to Officer Gibson. "What you told me is that this five-foot-three-inch woman attacked you with a carrot and a potbellied pig. Is that right?" Hugh couldn't believe what he was saying, or that that was what he'd have to say in court.

"Yes, sir."

The chief nodded at Bert.

"That's the way it happened," Len Hicks echoed.

Hugh sat back with a sigh. "Just for the record, let me tell you what's going to happen if we go to court with this. First, as you should know, Miss Simms will find legal representation."

The men grinned and then gave each other a high five.

In fact, the chief appeared to be the only one who realized what Hugh had said.

"Miss Simms' attorney will tell the jury that you, Mr. Hicks, wanted to kill and eat that tiny little pig. That will make you look like

someone who might go into the jurors' neigh-
borhoods and eat their cats and dogs."

A frown replaced Len's haughty expression.

Hugh then took on the policeman. "And all
your department buddies are going to wonder
why you let a woman that petite take you
down."

The officer, too, looked displeased.

"Guys, I want to help you." It was only half
a lie. Had anyone really been hurt, he'd be glad
to help him. "I want to see justice served—it's
why I came to work here on the DA's office.
However, you don't have a case. Let's drop
these charges and move on with our lives,
okay?"

The men's gazes locked for a long moment,
as if they were deciding together what to do.

"It's okay, boys." The chief opened the
door. "The department is completely behind
you." With that, he was gone.

Finally Officer Gibson spoke. "My name's
been on TV the past few weeks. Everyone
knows I was assaulted."

"And what about me?" Len asked. "The
woman down the block said she'd never dated
a man who had witnessed a crime. If we drop
these charges, what will happen?"

Hugh expected this; no one ever wanted to

drop charges once the press got involved. "You'll tell everyone that the DA's office said there wasn't enough evidence to indict." He stood.

The other men did not.

Len piped up. "You're not going to make us look stupid, are you, Mr. Cramer?"

"Well, guys, you're doing that pretty well on your own. Will you listen to yourselves? Every time you tell the story, it gets a little bit bigger. But in essence both of you admit that a woman kicked your butts. I'm sure your neighbor would love to date a guy a girl can beat up. Besides, you can't win this case."

Gibson raised himself out of his chair. "I'll just tell you this. With the department behind me, I'm going to see that woman in jail for what she did. She isn't going to make a fool out of me."

They both got up and left, grumbling all the way.

Chapter Four

When the interviews were over, Hugh thought the day couldn't get any worse.

Until his boss stopped by to pay him a visit.

"Walter," he said, "we aren't really taking this to court, right? Though it appears Chief Cary has some hand in the situation. Please tell me we're not going to prosecute this."

"We have to," his boss replied grimly.

"Excuse me?"

Uneasiness etched itself over Walter's craggy features. "You heard what I said."

"I wish I hadn't. Once Kendra Simms gets a lawyer, these guys will never hold up under cross."

"So get her to plead out, and get this over

61

with." He rubbed his eyes with one hand. "I've already gotten some heat over this."

"Listen to me. We can't take this into court. Regardless of what the chief wants you to do."

"We have to try her. No more argument." Walter left Hugh's office with his usual confident stride.

Why shouldn't he be confident? It was Hugh whose reputation would get dumped into the toilet after this farce of a trial.

Lydia came in with some messages and a cold drink. "You okay?"

"No. I'm in deep."

"Yeah. It's all over the office. But if anyone can fix this, you can."

Hugh grinned warily at the pretty blond. "Thanks for the vote of confidence. If I'm going to fix it, I'd better get some duct tape." He leaned back in his chair. "Lots and lots of duct tape."

"No, Grandma. Really, I'm okay."

Kendra's grandmother called weekly from Florida to check up on her and encourage her to find a husband.

"Kendra, your sister is three years younger than you are. She's married, she's got a baby, and she's living in her own house, not a basement. Not that you don't have your mother's basement fixed up like the cutest little apartment, but still. Now, I try not to hold her up to you as an example, but, honey, don't you ever look at her life and think, that would work for me too?"

Kendra didn't let her grandmother know how her comments made her feel. "I am happy for Mishel, but we're different. Sure, I'd like the white picket fence as much as anyone, but right now I'm where I am."

"According to your local newspaper, which we still subscribe to down here, you've been arrested again."

"Wait until you see the tape I'm sending you of what really happened." She explained that Pete Randall had given her a copy of her confrontation with the Clinton Heights Community Organization.

"You know, as your grandmother, I should keep fussing at you, but as someone who believes in what you do, I hope you overnighted it."

Her grandparents always came around to her way of thinking. Eventually.

"What's next?" Grandma asked gleefully.

" 'Next' is running the shelter, finding homes for the animals, and continuing my work."

"So that cute prosecutor has your case again, huh?"

Kendra smiled, even though no one was there to see it. "He's really a nice guy in a bad situation. Politics are playing into this, and he has no control over that."

"Sounds to me like you like him."

"He can be a pain, but he's done some things for me he'd get into trouble for if anyone knew."

"Which could mean he likes you as well?"

Kendra hesitated. "Yeah, I think so. But you make me feel guilty, saying it out loud."

Grandma giggled like a schoolgirl. "Hey, he's cute, he's got a good job, and he's a nice guy. Sounds like a grandmother-in-law's dream, if you ask me."

"Let's not get carried away."

"No, honey. *Do* get carried away. I want you to be happy. I know the animals do some of that for you, but I want to see you sharing your life with someone."

Grandma's earlier words still hurt. "Someone like Mishel's husband, John."

"Heavens, no! You and John would kill each other in two weeks. I want you to have someone suited to you. A man who understands you and loves you and wants to grow old with you. Doesn't every grandmother want those things for her grandbabies?"

Kendra went from hurt to guilt. "I suppose so."

"I'm proud of you, Kendra. Your granddad and I brag all the time about your work and your courage. But I want you to be careful. This is a real criminal charge. Have you got someone you trust representing you?"

Kendra couldn't lie, but she couldn't exactly tell the truth either. "I . . . do. I . . . trust this person as much as I trust myself."

"Good. Remember, little girl, your granddad and I follow the news closely."

"I won't forget."

"I need to go, sweetie. I love you."

"Love you back."

They rang off.

Kendra needed to get ready for the board meeting tonight. Usually she looked forward to seeing the board, made up mostly of her friends, but she was a little anxious that her latest court case wasn't being accepted well. Also, she needed to confront the members regarding Vickie Sawyer's statement that the board might not renew her contract. The pay and benefits weren't much, but they were all she had.

She dressed in a suit and went to the bank's boardroom, where the meetings had been held since the Rescue started more than five years earlier.

She did her usual ooh-ing and ah-ing over pictures of children and pets and found herself more relaxed than when she came in.

Harold Frey, the president of the board, called the meeting to order. The minutes of the last meeting were read and approved, as was the treasurer's report.

Some old business, not of much consequence, was discussed, and under new business, Kendra was asked to talk about her case.

"It is merely a ruse to hurt the Rescue," she said simply.

A member raised a hand to ask a question. "Kendra, can you think of why someone would do that?"

"I can tell you that the chief of police just moved to Clinton Heights, which is right next door to us. I'm wondering if some of the residents there dislike having an animal shelter so close to them."

There were murmurings amid the board members.

"I can see that, but to try to have you jailed over it doesn't make sense."

"I don't want to come off as arrogant, but some people in the community see me as the Rescue."

There was no disagreement.

Kendra took the atmosphere of concurrence to broach the dreaded topic. "Vickie Sawyer said that one of you told her I might be fired over this."

"I was the one she contacted," Frey admitted. "She asked me if your contract was up anytime soon, and I told her it was."

"Did you tell her the board might not renew it?"

"I did no such thing. I told her the publicity you generated was sometimes negative but it was always helpful in the end."

The room became quiet for a long moment.

Mr. Frey spoke in hushed tones to the secretary of the board.

The secretary, Mrs. Stevens, raised her hand. "I move we no longer give any comments to Channel Seven news or Miss Sawyer, as she cannot be just in her reporting."

The motion carried unanimously. The board would give a no-comment to anyone from Channel Seven.

That would help Kendra's case immensely, since it was so obvious that Vickie Sawyer had some bone to pick with her. The meeting soon came to an end.

As Kendra got into her car, her cell phone rang.

"Kendra, it's Hugh."

"Oh?" Kendra froze with her key in midair. What could he want?

"Have you eaten yet?" he asked.

"No, but—"

"You know where the Plainsville exit is on I-40?"

"Sure. Why?"

"And the convenience mart near there too?"

"Do you mean the one with the specially-made–doughnut commercials on the radio?"

"Right. Meet me there in twenty minutes."

"Why?"

"Because I'm saying please."

Two voices warred in her mind. One screamed, *Don't! Don't! This can't be good!*

The other said, *You get to see him!*

She thought about her earlier conversation with Grandma. "I'll be there."

Her pulse raced as she started the car and maneuvered into downtown traffic.

Chapter Five

At the store, Hugh had parked his late-model sedan to one side, out of view of most customers. She pulled in next to it. With a bag in hand, he immediately got into Kendra's SUV.

He took hot dogs and soft drinks from the bag.

"My, my, Mr. Cramer, I didn't know you'd be taking me to such an elegant dinner."

"It was this or those really awful sausages that they've cooked forever. I didn't like the look of them."

She put a little mustard on her hot dog and chomped down. She hadn't realized how hungry she was. "Either this is really good, or I'm starving."

Hugh sipped his drink from a straw. "I think it's the latter."

After a few moments of small talk Kendra asked, "Tell me why you called me here tonight."

"Several reasons really. But only one matters." His eyes held a flame. "I can't get your green eyes out of my mind. They should name that color after you."

Okay, so it was a line. But it was a good line, and she couldn't help but be flattered. "So, there would be people with Kendra-colored eyes?"

"Oh, yeah."

"I like that."

"Me too."

For something to fill the quiet Kendra told him, "I thought you might like to know, my showing on the eleven o'clock news has me receiving fan e-mail."

"What does that mean?"

"It means Chief Cary's ambush worked out for me in the media, and I'm getting e-mail from people encouraging me to continue helping the animals."

He reached out and took her hand. "I'm in so much trouble that a special meeting is being called tomorrow just to discuss your case."

"You don't appear upset."

"That's because I'm more concerned . . ." His voice trailed off as he fumbled for words. ". . . with you—and the shelter, of course. I don't want to see anything bad happen to either one of you."

She tried to focus on her words, not the tension mounting in the car, tension that had nothing to do with lawsuits or potbellied pigs. "I've been through thorny legal issues in the past. The time we rescued those cats from that woman who was abusing them was worse than this, Hugh."

Hugh absently stroked her thumb. "That time you got very positive publicity. But for some reason you've really ticked off Vickie Sawyer. Any ideas on that?"

She filled with warmth from his touch but held her voice steady. "She came down hard on me when I got the job at the shelter. I think—to be honest with you—it had to do with the Fairmont Farms—now the Sommars'—pig." She cocked her head to one side in thought. "Which really doesn't make much sense."

He leaned across the console and kissed her ever so gently. "I've been wanting to do that for a while now. I hope you don't mind."

She took a deep breath. "I don't mind." Her

voice a whisper, she asked, "Is it okay that I've wanted you to?"

His disarming smile made her weak. "I think so."

The dark car, parked away from the hustle and bustle of the store, was a perfect place to kiss and nuzzle in private. The only problem was the console.

And, of course, the fact that they shouldn't be there at all.

She leaned into him as much as the car would allow and didn't want him to quit holding her. Not ever.

Between kisses Hugh murmured, "You know Sawyer was the person Fairmont was having an affair with at the time, don't you?"

"Who?" she asked dreamily.

He pulled ever so slightly away. "Sawyer."

"Oh, her," she said absently.

His lips captured hers again. His kisses were confident but sweet. Even her toes grew warm.

"How did you know that?" she asked, belatedly rousing herself to full consciousness.

He pulled away, took a couple of deep breaths, and smiled at her. His hair, disheveled from her running her fingers through it, only added to his allure. "You drive me nuts. I can't wait until this is all over."

She cleared her throat in an effort to pull herself together. "If it helps any, I feel the same way."

Pulling her as close as he could over the console, he told her the rest of the story. "Back to your question, it hit the media right after the Fairmonts' divorce became final. Sallie Fairmont, who took her money and headed to Bermuda, made sure the press got wind of the affair. Sawyer almost lost her job over it."

"That still doesn't answer what I had to do with anything."

"Well, your protests brought the Fairmonts media scrutiny. Maybe you stirred things up and bring back bad memories for her."

"Did she and Fairmont break up?"

"Yup. A few months later he took off to Vegas, found a showgirl, and remarried almost immediately. I heard that they're doing really well, though. Had a kid and everything."

Both of them fell silent and began cleaning up the remnants of their meal, putting all the wrappers into the bag it came in.

"It's hard for me to believe I'm sitting here with you," Kendra said shyly.

Their lips touched briefly. "Like I said, sweetie, you are driving me insane. You're beautiful, you're smart, and you've got convictions."

"And maybe will *be* convicted," she said wryly.

"I hope it doesn't come to that. But you know I have to do my job."

Her heart fell. "I know. You're a man of convictions too. That's one of the reasons I feel so strongly about you."

"I like the sound of that."

They kissed again, her emotions running wild with his touch.

He pulled back only far enough to speak, his voice husky. "I need to go. Heaven only knows how much trouble I'd be in if anyone saw us. But, Kendra, you have to know I don't want to go."

"We've met on cases before. Why this one?"

"I wish I knew." He kissed her again.

When he finished, her voice was barely a whisper. "So we're back to square one." Emotions flooded through her as she thought of all the things that kept them apart—the politics, the case, the Rescue. Dear God, what was she thinking?

"I guess we are. And I need to stay away from you until after this all blows over."

"Okay." Disappointment trickled through her. "I understand."

With a reluctant motion he pulled back completely to his side of the console. "If you'd get a lawyer, this could be over much sooner."

He kissed her quickly and was gone.

Hugh waited in the conference room for Walter, tapping his pen on the big table and wondering how this would go. His boss had been furious when he called the meeting, so Hugh knew he was in really deep and wasn't sure even duct tape could help him.

Walter entered the room and closed the door. "Cary is all over me. You want to tell me what happened?" he demanded as he took a seat.

"He wanted me to comment on a case that's still under investigation," Hugh replied.

"We're talking about Kendra Simms again, aren't we?"

Hugh explained what had happened at the Clinton Heights clubhouse the evening the press showed and Kendra knocked Cary's socks off with her side of the story.

"I know you're under pressure, Walter, but you need to rethink what you're doing. If Kendra Simms gets an attorney—forget that, if she defends herself the way she did the other night—we can't beat her."

"We can't beat an amateur defending herself? You must not be as big a hotshot as you thought you were."

Hugh studied Walter for a moment. Then he heard words coming out of his own mouth he didn't expect. "No, actually, I'm probably better than I claim to be. But when a woman points out that she stands only five-three and that if she can whip a cop, we'd better get different ones, she's right."

Walter sat back in his chair and shook his head. "This should have been an easy case. We should have gotten her to plead out, do a little community service, maybe pay a small fine, and get it over with."

"Instead, your pal on the police force has made this into exactly what I feared—a circus," Hugh replied grimly.

"The mayor called me yesterday too. He's fit to be tied."

"There's the tightwire act. You know, the one that tears up your nerves while you're waiting for the fall." Hugh smirked. "On top of it I have a case based on the testimony of the clowns."

"And Cary's the ringmaster," Walter said grimly.

"Right." Then Hugh wondered aloud, "What would you do if it were all up to you?"

"I'd drop this case and tell Marvin Cary to find another way to close the Rescue."

"The guy might live in Clinton Heights,

where the shelter is, but he's crazy if he thinks the people of this city—our potential jury—will do anything against that shelter."

Walter cursed under his breath. "This is all about property values, then."

"I didn't realize it until I attended Chief Cary's little roast of Kendra Simms."

Walter took a deep breath but didn't say anything.

Hugh took a chance. "I suppose we could drop the charges."

"I can talk to the mayor." Walter stood up to leave. "Of course, he has property up there too. I don't see any way out of this one, Hugh. Just do it."

Hugh got up as well. "I hate the politics. Walter, I know this leaves you between a rock and a hard place, but I think you're allowing this to go too far. Tell them the way it is, and we can all get on with our lives."

"That's easier said than done, Hugh. There's a lot of money invested in Clinton Heights."

"Since I've been here, I've been accused of wanting your job. I don't. But this situation makes me wonder if it wouldn't be better if someone else did run next year."

Walter's face reddened. "I can't believe you said that."

"This is a farce. End it, Walter. *That's* your

job." Hugh left him and went to his office. When he arrived, he closed his door and leaned against it, closing his eyes. *I can't believe I just said that.*

Chapter Six

"I can't thank you enough for coming to see me so quickly, Miss Simms."

Kendra shook the offered hand of Beth Chambers-Price. She found herself in a small Trentville medical clinic about forty-five minutes from Fort White.

"I can only thank *you*," she said as she sat down opposite the other woman, "for seeing me. Please call me Kendra."

"And call me Beth." The woman's attire, from business suit to gold earrings, looked elegant and classy. And the woman had married Danni's brother, a doctor. "My understanding is that you have several dogs and cats you need homes for."

"That's correct," Kendra replied.

"Let me tell you a little bit about what I do. I'm the administrator of the Thompson-Price Wellness Clinic. Are you familiar with us?"

"Danni told me a little. I can't say that I know much, except that a few years ago you broke off from the local hospital."

"That's right. Our clinic works with grants, sliding fee scales, and anything else we can to help the indigent and uninsured of the community."

Already Kendra loved the place. How wonderful for people to care so much and not expect to become wealthy in return. "It sounds like a fantastic concept, but what does this have to do with the Seaton Animal Rescue?"

"We also provide pet therapy for our patients. Do you know much about that?"

"Recently I've learned a little about it."

"That's right. You have Danni and Michael's pig, Joey, helping you with a little potbelly of your own. Joey's great with people too. How's that going for you?" Beth's candid look said she truly listened.

"Hamlette is doing much better. I'm hoping this week, in fact, to start letting her out of her cage for a few minutes at a time."

"I'm sure you're glad of that."

"Very."

"Well, here's my proposal for you." She handed Kendra a packet in a blue report cover. "This has all the information you'll need. When you take in strays, we ask you to see whether they meet the criteria in this. If you think they do, we'll send over Dr. Darlene Thompson, who has become a nationally known expert on the use of pet therapy. She'll also examine the animal and possibly bring him here for a few days or a week."

"So you really want to take *my* animals and put them to work in pet therapy?" It would mean another great avenue toward finding homes for her strays.

"That's right."

"But they're not purebreds. They're usually mutts and strays."

Beth put down her pen. "If they're friendly with people, they could be used."

Kendra couldn't help but be excited. "I have quite a few animals right now that I think would be great for this. The type that respond beautifully to people."

"Perfect. We'll send Darlene Thompson over as soon as we can put your schedules together."

After a knock on the door, it opened. A man in a white lab coat with dark hair and glasses entered. "How's it going?"

"This is Kendra Simms from the Seaton Animal Rescue," Beth answered him, "and she's excited about our taking some of her animals. Kendra, meet my husband, Dr. Alex Price."

Alex Price shook her hand. His shake was firm, and his brown eyes danced as if he knew a funny secret he'd never share. "Call me Alex. You ever get any big snakes or exotic animals?"

"We have in the past."

"I know a few annoying patients I'd like to send *those* to."

Kendra joined in on the joke. "So instead of bringing down their blood pressure, you want to give them a stroke?"

He winked at her. "You catch on fast."

"I had an alligator once. Would that have done the trick?"

He crossed his arms over his chest, tilting his head to one side. "What did you do with it?"

"A zoo in Wisconsin took him."

"Alex?" Beth grinned. "Before you have to go, I wanted you to know the Strongs grant went through."

He grabbed his wife at the elbows. "You can't be serious. You said the chances were slim to none."

Beth's mouth curved with tenderness for her husband. "I can be wrong on occasion. Of course, not often."

He kissed her right there in front of Kendra. "Do you realize what this will mean?"

She nodded. "More of our patients can get medications for free."

Before he could comment further, he was paged overhead to the phone. "Back to earth. When do I pick up the Menacing Munchkins?"

"When your shift ends at four. Of course, for you that means four-thirty or closer to five."

"You slay me with your humor."

"And the truth?"

He threw her a kiss. "Love ya. And, Kendra, great meeting you. Danni had only good things to say about you." He exited the room.

Kendra had to know. "The Menacing Munchkins?"

Beth picked up a framed photo from her desk and handed it to Kendra. "They're almost two years old." Beautiful identical twin boys in matching suits smiled back at her. "They are the sweetest and most conniving children who ever walked the earth."

Kendra gave the portrait back to Beth.

"Whenever Dr. Thompson is available, I will be too. Just call me."

"Thanks, Kendra. I'll do that."

Hugh knew that he'd soon run out of options if he couldn't get Kendra to plead to something. Further discussion with Walter had become a living nightmare; he was either to plead her out or prosecute her and win.

Win! Win with the officer who thought he'd been assaulted with a carrot, and his pal, who told him it was cool having his name announced on television.

Then there was Chief Cary.

He'd obviously decided that demolishing Kendra was the best way to get the Rescue out of his classy new neighborhood. And that's exactly why Hugh was in the position he was.

Hugh sat back in his chair. He took a long moment to think about the situation. If Cary was the problem, then that's where he needed to begin, not with his witness, so-called victim, or the judge.

As he picked up the phone to dial, Lydia opened his door. "Miss Simms is here to see you, Mr. Cramer."

"Send her in." He stood and buttoned his jacket, then shook Kendra's offered hand. As glad as he was to see her, he just knew that something was rattling around in that pretty head of hers.

Kendra had an amused gleam in her eye that said he was in for a Kodak moment. "Mr. Cramer."

"Miss Simms. Won't you sit down?"

She sat opposite him. "I have filed a motion to dismiss the charges against me."

He cocked his head and asked, "On what grounds, Miss Simms?"

"When I was arrested, I wasn't read my rights."

"According to the police statement, you were read your rights."

She handed him the motion on paper. "I disagree with that finding and will ask for a dismissal."

Hugh leaned forward. "You are making my life miserable on so many different levels. Plead no contest, and I'll get you thirty hours of community service and your record expunged when it's completed."

"Are you kidding? No way. I'm on a roll. I've made Cary look like a complete idiot. I've made the cop look like a horse's—" She searched the room with her gaze, as if looking for a polite word. "Well, you know. Anyway, so far I'm winning. Why would I quit now?"

He took a deep breath. "For me?"

"Hmm. That is on a different level, I admit." She scrunched her nose and acted as though she were giving the matter lots of thought. "No. I'm not giving in. Not yet."

"You know we go to court in three days."

"Know?" She got up to leave. "I'm so excited, I'm considering inviting everyone I've ever met!"

"I'm actually a pretty good prosecutor when I'm not thinking about you, and I might just have a few tricks up my sleeve you aren't aware of."

She leaned on the desk with both hands and got close enough that he could feel her breath on his face. "Unless you have David Copperfield up your sleeve, I'm good to go."

She brought herself up straight. "See you on the courthouse steps, big guy." With that, she was gone, leaving behind a motion to dismiss and the light fragrance of wildflowers.

He wasn't sure if he wanted to strangle her or kiss her into submission.

As if.

Shock poured through Hugh when Danni Sommars walked into the hearing with Kendra. *This is all I need.* "So you got an attorney," he said to Kendra.

Danni interrupted any answer she might

have given. "Yes. Much as I hate criminal law, I talked her into letting me take over."

"As a favor to the shelter, Ms. Sommars is working pro bono, which did away with any objections I had to acquiring counsel," Kendra smugly told him as she walked to her seat.

"All rise!" the bailiff called as Judge Cole came into the room.

He sat down and glared at Hugh, who looked away. *He's going to kill me when this is over.*

After studying all parties involved, Judge Cole called Hugh to his chambers.

Danni left her seat and walked to the front of the defense table. "Your Honor, if there's a problem with my client's case, I have the right to hear what you and Mr. Cramer discuss."

The judge glared at Danni, who brazenly smiled and wrinkled her nose at him.

"Don't you dare think, young lady, that just because you're my granddaughter-in-law, I won't toss you into jail for contempt and throw away the key."

Hugh didn't dare move.

Trying to hide her amused expression, Danni dropped her gaze to the floor.

"However," the judge said to the courtroom, "since Ms. Sommars is correct to protect her client's rights, I ask that she and Mr. Cramer join me at the bench for a sidebar."

Danni walked toward the judge.

"Mr. Cramer," he whispered, "I thought this was going to go away quietly."

Just then Fort White's most annoying news-woman, Vickie Sawyer, walked through the door. She'd had the good sense to leave her cameraman outside; she'd been around Fort White long enough to know that Judge Cole didn't put up with cameras in his courtroom.

The judge's eyes narrowed on Kendra, who, in Hugh's opinion, wisely gave nothing away.

"Miss Simms, did you call the media?" the judge asked her.

"No, sir, I did not."

"So you're surprised to see them here?"

"Miss Sawyer follows me like a stray dog. Why should anything she does surprise me?"

The judge took a deep breath and exhaled slowly. Hugh knew him well enough to know that he was counting to ten.

Danni didn't hesitate to face the judge squarely. "Your Honor, I suggest you dis-miss this case and save the taxpayers some money."

Don't push him. Whatever you do, don't push, Hugh thought.

"Ms. Sommars, is there any reason you can think of as to why you and Mr. Cramer cannot come to a satisfactory compromise?"

"Yes, sir." She didn't continue but waited to be asked.

She's going to push Cole until he cracks, Hugh realized.

"Would you like to share it with me, or shall I ask that the news cameras be turned on first?"

"My client refuses to plead out in light of the fact that she did nothing wrong and, upon arrest, was not read her rights."

"Mr. Cramer, are the People ready to proceed?"

"We are, Your Honor."

"Then, against *my* better judgment, it looks like we'll have a hearing. Both of you, sit down."

As both Hugh and Danni returned to their seats, he found himself watching the chief of police's arrival. Something stank in Denmark, and the courtroom was beginning to get a bit ripe as well.

Hugh nodded in such a way that Danni glanced behind her. Her eyes told him she understood his concern.

Danni whispered something to Kendra, but Hugh couldn't do or say anything more.

"We're waiting on the People, Mr. Cramer." The judge peered at Hugh over his glasses. That was never a good sign.

"The People call Officer Bert Gibson to the stand."

Danni again stood. "Your Honor."

"Yes, Ms. Sommars?"

"I don't believe the court has properly evaluated my client's motion to dismiss."

"As a matter of fact, I have. If she'd had an attorney to start with, she wouldn't have wasted the court's time with this. When she told the arresting officer that she knew her rights, that was all he needed."

Danni sat back down and nodded to Kendra. She'd been around long enough, Hugh knew, that she'd known what would happen, but it was still worth a try. Under the circumstances, he probably would have done the same thing.

The judge's flat tone filled the room. "Continue, Mr. Cramer."

Bert was sworn in and asked to recall the incident in his own words.

"I was driving my patrol car through town when I heard on my radio that there was a man behind the Village Ridge subdivision with a gun. I went there and found Miss Simms and Mr. Hicks fighting over a pig."

The judge sat straight up. "Did you say a pig?"

"I did, Your Honor."

Cole waved a dismissive hand. "Should've known. Go on."

"Well, Len—that is, Mr. Hicks—had decided the animal was a menace, and he wanted to kill it. Miss Simms disagreed and brought out a carrot to try to catch the thing."

"And you were hurt in the ensuing fight?" Hugh asked him.

"The pig ran through my legs, and when she went after it, I was knocked down. She showed no respect for me at all." He appeared well pleased with himself.

"Thank you, Officer Gibson." Hugh waved toward Danni. "Your witness."

"Thank you." Danni rose and approached the witness box. "Officer Gibson, did Miss Simms threaten you that day?"

"No." He tensed in his seat.

Danni kept her cool. "Did *she* have a gun?"

"No. But she stabbed me in the leg with a carrot."

The judge banged his gavel as the spectators in the courtroom burst into laughter. Cole was beyond angry, Hugh saw in his steel gray eyes. The judge was furious. "Officer Gibson, is this the best you have to say to this court? That you were hurt by a carrot wielded by a woman half your size, who you admit did not hurt you intentionally?"

"She stabbed me with—"

The judge waved away his statement and turned to Hugh. "Can the People manufacture a case or not, counselor?"

"Your Honor, I understand your frustration. But please remember that many times assaults are committed with objects not thought of as usual. A screwdriver can stab. A trophy can be used to bludgeon someone. I could go on and on. The People have a viable case, Your Honor. Please hear us out."

A deep breath from the judge told Hugh that he was skating on thin, incredibly thin, ice.

"Okay. But something better than this story had better surface. Fast."

"Thank you, Your Honor." *Tissue-thin ice.*

"Defense may continue," Cole pronounced.

Danni's condescending questions stopped right there. "I see no reason to go further, Your Honor. I believe this court understands the true situation."

"Your Honor, if I may, I'd like to redirect," Hugh said.

"By all means." The words were standard, but the tone told Hugh that, if possible, the ice beneath his feet was melting by the minute.

"Office Gibson, would you say that when this happened, Miss Simms was at all remorseful?"

"She didn't care I was hurt, if that's what you mean. She was mad."

"Mad? At you?"

"Well, yes. Like I'd been in her way, or something."

"So, you were hurt, and she didn't care?"

Danni waved a hand. "Objection. Calls for speculation. There isn't any way the officer could know what Miss Simms was feeling."

"I'll rephrase." Hugh got serious. If he had to try this case, he'd give it everything. "When you got up from the ground, did Miss Simms help you up, did she apologize, did she say she was sorry?"

Gibson, still sheepish after the earlier exchange, spoke quietly. "She helped me up. But like I said, she yelled at me. Told me I'd gotten in her way."

"So you're saying you were assaulted because she'd stop at nothing to get to the pig."

The officer straightened in his chair. "Yes."

Danni leaned over and whispered to Kendra. He was surprised she hadn't objected.

"Did she give you a reason for her behavior?"

"Not really."

"Thank you, Officer Gibson. I appreciate you sharing your story."

"You may step down," Judge Cole said solemnly. As if maybe the officer's testimony did prove something. Or at least would.

Len Hicks was sworn in next, and after he took the stand, Hugh asked him the same standard questions, receiving mostly the same answers.

But on cross-examination Danni threw the proverbial monkey wrench into the mix. "Mr. Hicks, you say that the officer just did his job and this all ended that day as it should have."

The man had a confident air. "That's right."

"Why were you out there in the wooded area anyway?"

He stammered, "I-I . . . well . . . I was looking for the pig too."

"Didn't you see how small he was, that he was a pet pig?"

"A pig is a pig to me. I'm not a fancy person who sees pigs as pets. They're farm animals or wild, is all."

"More precisely, you saw the little gal as food, didn't you?"

Judge Cole banged his gavel as the courtroom filled with murmurs of disgust.

Hugh just lost the case, and he knew it.

The judge threw his glasses onto the desk and rubbed his eyes. "Mr. Cramer?"

"Yes, Your Honor?"

"This case is dismissed. You tell Walter Henry that I want him in my chambers in"—he checked his watch—"two hours. If he's not there, I'll have an officer come to escort him. Do you understand me?"

"Yes, Your Honor."

"Good. Miss Simms, I'm retiring in a couple of months. Do you think you can stay out of trouble until I'm off the bench?"

"I'll try, sir."

"See to it that you do."

Chapter Seven

Outside the courtroom, Vickie Sawyer had a tough time trying to destroy Kendra when she'd already been exonerated. Of course, Kendra didn't try to make the woman's life any easier in the interview she gave. What Sawyer didn't know was that Kendra was on her way to Pete Randall's television station, where he awaited her for an exclusive interview.

This is the best day! Kendra thought triumphantly.

When she hugged Danni and asked her to join her, Danni reminded Kendra that her relationship with Mr. Randall wasn't the best and left for home.

As she opened her car door, she sensed a presence behind her and knew who it would be. She spoke quietly. "Hey there."

"You realize, of course, that for you this is over, but I am in deep—"

"I'm sorry. But, Hugh, honestly, I'm right about this."

"I know." He paused. "I really want to see you."

She couldn't help the smile that tugged at the corners of her mouth. "Me too."

"But we've got to wait awhile before being seen together."

Her heart fell. "I suppose we should."

"Well, I'd better go face the music."

"Yeah. And I've got an interview to get to."

She watched him turn and walk away, and she ached to be with him.

When she got into the SUV, she checked her cell phone messages.

The only message she had was from Hugh. "Danni's going to have you over to her place this weekend, and I'll be there too. I can't wait to see you. This way it will look casual instead of like we're dating. I don't like the lie, hon, but under the circumstances, I have to be careful. I hope you understand. I'll call you tonight. It may be a little late, after nine. Take care of yourself and that pig, okay? Bye."

Almost giddy from hearing that he'd called and would be seeing her soon, she started the car and rolled into traffic. This day was just getting better and better.

After hours of deliberations and arguments, Hugh had had enough. "If this day doesn't get any better, I'm going to stab *myself* with a carrot."

Despite himself, Judge Cole chuckled. "Hugh's right, Walter. We can sit here and discuss this all night, but the truth is, you did this to please Marvin Cary, and that is not going to work in my courtroom again."

Walter had made Hugh attend this command performance with him and had been on the defensive since arriving in the judge's chambers. "Let me say this, Judge. You need to talk to the chief as well. You've put me on the chopping block, but I'm not retiring in a couple of months like you are. I'm here for the duration."

"I'll buy that. If you're reelected, that is." The judge checked his watch. "I'm late for supper at Danielle's. She's another one who gets to hear from me this evening."

Hugh thought about Danni. She'd get the talking to of her life, knowing the judge. "You know she just wanted to help Kendra."

With a weary glance at Hugh, Walter asked,

"All of a sudden you two are on a first-name basis?"

The judge also questioned him. "How did she and Danni come to know each other, anyway? Did you introduce them?"

"It was the pigs." Not a complete lie, Hugh reminded himself. "Danni heard about the pig, and she decided to help Kendra." He realized he sounded guilty. "I mean, you know Danni loves her potbellied pig, and when she heard that someone with a pig like hers needed help . . ."

"I'll ask her all about it tonight. For now you're free to go."

Hugh hadn't fooled the good judge, and he knew it. As he reached his car, he called Danni to warn her about the third degree she'd get when the judge arrived.

"Don't worry about us," Danni told him. "We'll still be family when all this is over. You worry about you and Kendra and how you're going to see her in the next few months without catching flack."

He did worry.

But that didn't mean he wouldn't see her Saturday night.

Candles in beautiful hummingbird lanterns hung from wrought iron poles throughout

Danni's front yard and along the walk to her open door.

Inside, Kendra could see that the den tables had snacks awaiting all those who entered. What a great party this would be, Kendra thought.

And Hugh would be here.

Kendra did the one thing that scared her. She set the carrier she held onto the foyer floor. No signs of agitation from within. No signs of biting, gnawing on the bars, or any other aggression. Could it be that Joey had done the trick?

Speaking of whom, he came out of the den to investigate the newcomers to the party. He licked at the cage in which Hamlette rested, and with a deep breath Kendra opened it.

Hamlette stood up and walked toward Joey. They trotted through the house together as if to show off their friendship.

Kendra released her breath and smiled broadly when Hugh sidled up beside her with an extra cup of punch. "Looks like someone else found a girlfriend through all my trials and tribulations."

She nodded as she took the offered glass and sipped her drink. "I think they—and we—have a good thing going," she said a little shyly.

"I agree. This is the countdown. We count sixty days from the court date, and after that we go public. That is if . . ." His voice trailed off.

Her stomach lurched. "If?"

He glanced around the room, making sure they were alone. "If I can wait that long." He kissed her gently just as the front door opened.

"What's this?" Judge Cole's voice rang throughout the house, bringing others from the den and kitchen.

Even the pigs came to see what the commotion was.

Busted. There was no other word for it.

Hugh didn't falter. Instead, he faced down the judge. "I'm merely enjoying Miss Simms' company."

The judge, the perfect Southern gentleman, refrained from saying anything insulting to or about Kendra. "I can see that. I can also understand why you'd want to. However, weren't you her prosecutor earlier this week?"

"But I'm not now."

"I see. Well"—he cleared his throat—"Danielle, I believe I was invited here for dinner."

Danni stepped away from the others. "Yes, Judge. If you'll join us in the den, I'm serving appetizers there."

The judge nodded to Kendra and retreated

after his hostess. The others, about six couples, joined him.

The pigs stayed. Hamlette lay down on Kendra's shoes.

"It's okay, girl. It's okay."

Kendra shot Hugh a glance. "You could be brought up in front of some kind of ethics committee because of me."

"I'm not backing away now."

She stepped back. "But I am. You're a brilliant attorney with a great career ahead of you. I'm not seeing you again, Hugh. Not for a while."

Hugh's eyes widened in surprise. "Everyone knows now that we're together. What difference can it make?"

Danni walked into the room. "Are you both staying for dinner this time?"

"How's the judge?" Kendra asked.

Danni didn't try to beat around the bush. "Apparently he's upset. Do we know why?"

Hugh didn't hesitate. "He caught us kissing."

Danni slapped him on the arm. "You have to be more careful."

"Excuse me." All three noticed the judge returning to the room. "I'm afraid I may have offended Miss Simms. That was not my intent."

"It's okay, Judge. I can understand—"

"Actually, Miss Simms, it's not right for me

to walk into this house and tell you how you should live your life. But I also must question the case you were involved in. Mr. Cramer, you should have recused yourself."

Hugh cleared his throat. "Now isn't the time to talk about this, Judge Cole."

"Perhaps you're right. But we need to discuss this situation as soon as possible. Miss Simms, I know you were a victim in this case, but I must warn you. If people learned about this liaison, you could also be in trouble."

"I was just leaving, Judge." She peered longingly at Hugh.

Hugh wouldn't hear of it. "Kendra, you—"

"Don't, Hugh. The judge is making good sense. Not just for you, for both of us."

Hugh watched as she walked out the front door and down the steps and got into her SUV.

"Aren't you going after her?" Danni asked.

"No. Not now. The judge and I need to have that talk first."

The judge agreed. "Danielle, if you'll excuse us."

Danni didn't question them as she left them alone.

"You have no right, Judge Cole. My case is finished. I'm on my own time."

"You come into my courtroom as a man of the law, while you're having an affair with the defendant? I have never been so disappointed in anyone."

That hurt.

"I'm not having an affair, and I can't believe you'd think I was. I just prosecuted her."

"You just kissed her when you thought no one was watching. That's the problem, Hugh. There's always someone watching. You are a talented attorney. I expect great things from you. But you've got to step back, for a while at least, if you're going to move up in your career."

"I think I'm in love with her."

"But that doesn't mean you can go around kissing her in public. You've got to show some restraint, man, or you'll fall flat on your face."

"What would you have me do? Would you have me ignore her? Treat her as if she doesn't exist?"

"I'm not the person to ask. You and she must come to a decision."

Hamlette and Joey came to lie at their feet.

"Looks like, Mr. Cramer, you have a pig to deliver."

At the Rescue, Kendra realized she'd left Hamlette at the party. She wasn't worried, of course. If anyone could keep a pig for a night, it was Danni. But she knew what she had to do.

"Hi." Hugh appeared at her office door, holding Hamlette's leash. "She did great. She's like a different animal."

"I know."

"I have your carrier. It's on the front step."

"Thank you."

"You know we need to talk."

"Yes. Let me put her into her cage."

He followed her, leading Hamlette by the leash to the kennel area.

Kendra faced him after putting the pig into her cage. Her sad eyes made him wonder if he could do what he had to do.

Then, in one second, he knew he couldn't.

"I had a decision to make."

"I know." Her voice held a sadness that broke his heart.

"I decided that I am going to have to do something else with my life, Kendra. I can't have you and a place at the DA's office. It just can't be done."

Her eyes became as wide as saucers. "You'd give up your job for me?"

He gently took her hand and kissed it. "To touch your hand, I'd give up everything I own."

With tears trickling down her cheeks, she told him, "I wouldn't ask that of you."

"You didn't. I made the decision on my own."

"But why?"

"Because I love the law, but it doesn't keep me warm at night. It's not as if I can't put out my own shingle. I just . . ." His voice trailed off.

"You just what?"

"I just want to be with you."

A long silence overtook them.

"There's one thing I don't know." He still held her hand.

"And that would be?"

"How you feel. Do you want to be with me, or is all this a moot point?"

"No. I definitely want to be with you."

He slowly bent to kiss her, his lips caressing hers. She loved the hum it sent through her entire body, making her toes curl.

When he pulled away, she felt cold and a little lonely. But the truth was, he couldn't give up a career he'd worked for all his life.

"I have a plan," she told him.

"Does it include any pigs?"

"No, but it does mean you won't give up everything you've done to get where you are."

He held her at arm's length. "You have that look in your eyes."

"My Kendra-colored eyes?"

"You liked that line, didn't you?"

"Oh, yeah." She tugged on his arm as she

began her proposal, leading him back toward the Rescue office. "We'll have to lay low for a while, but this is how we can do it and still keep our sanity."

"I'm all for that." He kissed her quickly before opening the door for her.

Chapter Eight

Kendra learned to live life outside the city limits.

Not wanting to jeopardize Hugh's position further, they did dinner and movies out of Fort White in the smaller suburban towns around it.

But dating Hugh wasn't her only problem.

After the nightmare she'd gone through with the Clinton Heights residents and the threat against the shelter and her own career, she felt the need to watch her back during every waking moment.

She found herself worried even if her car backfired or if the dogs barked for too long. Every move she made would be scrutinized from now on. And she had to protect the Rescue.

Hugh was always there for her.

Every night they weren't together, he'd call and reassure her that her position and the Rescue were assets to the community, and that the people in Fort White knew it and would protect her from anyone who tried to hurt her.

His words were always a comfort to her.

When they were together, he was the perfect date. Always attentive, always punctual, taking her to cozy restaurants and movies in out-of-the-way places where neither of them would be recognized.

However, no good thing can last forever.

Hugh and Kendra made a pact that they would be discreet for the next ninety days. They hoped that would give people time enough to forget. After three months, Kendra wasn't going to allow public opinion to stand in her way.

Danni had invited Kendra to the annual pet show at the county fair. Joey competed every year but had yet to win a first-place ribbon. It obviously stuck in Danni's craw as she told Kendra the story. "I always have him bow to the judges, but do they ever give him first prize? No. And Joey is beginning to resent it too."

The pigs lay sprawled across each other in the backseat of Danni's car. Michael would bring the kids, but Danni had Joey and picked up Kendra and Hamlette as well.

"I don't think he really understands," Kendra offered.

Danni gave her a sidelong glance. "I beg to differ, Miss Simms. My pig knows it all."

"Well, heaven forbid I question your pig, Mrs. Sommars," Kendra thought a moment. "After all, he's the reason you have your husband."

"And kids and the life I have now."

"I'll never question the little guy again."

"How's Hugh?"

Was Danni trying to be nonchalant in her change of subject? Kendra dropped her gaze to her cup holder. "How would I know?"

Danni pulled the car into the parking lot. "I wondered if you'd decided to take the judge's advice or not."

"Hugh admires Judge Cole. I can't imagine his doing anything to hurt him."

"Then you're still seeing him."

"What would make you think that?"

"You never answered my question." She parked the car. "Plus, you seem to know a lot about Hugh's feelings. That's always a sign." She faced her. "You want to talk about it?"

Avoiding the subject, Kendra told Danni, "I think we should get these kids inside."

"Be careful. Love can strike at the strangest hour."

Kendra opened her car door and took Hamlette's leash. It was unbelievable how easily she could handle the pig now that the gal had been calmed by the famous Joey.

Inside the arena where the pet show was held, Danni put the show collar around Joey's neck. He pranced in front of Hamlette, showing off for her.

Kendra laughed. "I'd never have believed that a pig could be a romantic!"

Danni shook her head. "The little guy can still amaze me too."

Kendra's breath stopped when she heard a voice behind her.

"Is he at it again?"

It was Hugh. She eyed him. Jeans and a blue pullover showed off his physique, and his smile melted her knees. *Good grief, I've got it so bad.*

"He's always up to something," Danni agreed.

"And, Miss Simms, I hope that this evening finds you well."

"Why, Mr. Cramer, thank you for asking.

It's a lovely evening to watch pigs prance, wouldn't you say?"

They found seats with Danni between them, waiting for Joey's turn to be called. Michael and the children came and sat behind them in the bleachers.

Cole and Leanne argued over the soft drinks Michael had purchased at the concession stand, but before anyone could settle the dispute, Joey was called. "And now, Joey the pot-bellied pig and his trainer, Danielle Sommars."

Joey did a little dance and some tricks and then bowed to all the judges, to the audience, and to Danni. Afterward he pranced by Hamlette again and sat down next to her.

As they all congratulated Danni and gave Joey a pat, Kendra felt a cold rush of liquid on her head and down her face. Ice and soda rushed down her, and she jumped up in shock.

Leanne screamed, "My drink! Cole took it and spilled it!"

"It was mine!" Cole answered. "Sorry, Miss Simms," he added as an afterthought.

"Was not!" Leanne started to cry.

Kendra wiped her face with one hand. "It's all right, you guys. Don't worry. I got to see Joey perform, and I'm leaving now anyway."

"I'm so sorry." Danni tried to dry her off

with tissues from her purse, and Michael raced back to the concession stand for napkins.

"It's fine, really. I'll go home and get cleaned up. See everyone later." Danni handed her keys to Kendra.

Kendra took hold of Hamlette's leash to leave, but Hugh followed her.

In the parking lot she put Hamlette into Danni's SUV. "I hope the commotion didn't hurt Joey's chances."

"I doubt it. Is being covered in cola the latest fashion for animal-shelter directors?"

She couldn't stop the giggle that popped out of her mouth.

He pulled her close and held her for a long moment. "I'm going to see how Joey's doing, then we can meet somewhere. That should give you time to clean up."

"Oh, Miss Simms!" The voice sounded too familiar.

Suddenly bright lights and camera flashes came out of nowhere.

Vickie Sawyer.

"Do you want to explain, Mr. Cramer, what you're doing kissing someone you just prosecuted not a month ago?"

Hugh grabbed Kendra's arm and steered her away from the media. "What in hell is she doing here?" he muttered.

Kendra had no answer for him.

"Sent here to cover a stupid pet show, and I find a real story! Tell me I'm not a great reporter!" She turned on her microphone. "So, tell me, Mr. Cramer, is it true that you purposely lost your prosecution of Miss Simms because you've been secretly seeing her?"

He held a hand up to shield him from the camera. He grabbed Kendra by one shoulder. "Get into the car and drive."

She obeyed without question. The one thing she didn't want was to face Vickie Sawyer right now.

She sped from the parking lot, trying not to draw attention to herself, but in her rearview mirror she could see Hugh attempting to get away from the media people who now encircled him.

Guilt engulfed her. *What could happen next?*

When the county fair came to town, every television station, radio personality, and newspaper covered the fun. She had tried to be careful but to no avail.

The throng of cameramen had found their way to where Hugh waited in the parking lot.

As people quieted to hear his remarks, he could only think, *what would the judge have me do?*

"Miss Simms and I are *now* friends but

were not when there were legal proceedings against her."

Questions came from all corners of the crowd. "So you're saying you broke up each time you prosecuted her?"

"No! Of course not. I—"

Another faceless voice asked, "So you've dated her for how long?"

"We didn't know each other personally before—"

Vickie Sawyer's voice cut through the group. "You're saying you fixed her cases for her favors?"

He'd had all he would take. "I'm leaving. Do not follow me."

He got into his car and drove away. *Now what would the judge say?*

Chapter Nine

"It's going to be okay."

Kendra sat on her mother's couch with her feet on the coffee table. "Then why hasn't he called me?"

"You know how the traffic is at the fair. Maybe he got stuck in it." Her mother continued to dust the house with a feather duster, knowing the whole time it would aggravate Kendra's allergies. But some things never change, and her mother was one of them.

"He has a cell phone. He could call me anytime. But it's been over an hour, and—"

The doorbell interrupted her soliloquy.

Her mother, instantly at the door, opened it,

and over her shoulder Kendra saw Hugh standing there.

"I'm sorry to barge in."

Kendra rose as her mother backed away from the door and allowed him to enter.

"Not a problem." Her mother nodded. "Kendra's friends are always welcome. You must be Hugh."

Although he answered the older woman, his eyes didn't leave Kendra's gaze. "That's right. It's nice to meet you, Mrs. Simms."

"Nice to meet you at last. As you can see, Kendra is here, and I must go dust the other room. You two can talk privately."

An uncomfortable silence lingered between them, but then Hugh took her into his arms. "I can't tell you how sorry I am about all this. It's actually already on the radio."

"I hate to see what happens on the eleven o'clock version of Miss Vickie."

"Call your buddy, Pete Randall, and see if he can do any damage control."

Good idea. She called the station and found that Pete was out of town.

"It's just not fair that Pete should think he can take off when I'm in a crisis. Perhaps, Hugh, you should let Danni and Michael know what happened. Maybe they'll come up with something we can do to fix this mess."

Before the words were out of her mouth, Hugh's cell phone rang. It was Danni, calling to report that Joey had won first prize in the pet show. Hugh gave the Sommars family his best wishes and hung up. "I can't tell them about this when they're on their way to celebrate."

They flopped down side by side on the couch.

"What's really the worst thing that could happen?" she finally asked.

"Really?" Hugh studied her a long moment. "Well, I guess embarrassment more than anything else. After all, we haven't done anything illegal."

"Then we just tell our friends and colleagues that we started seeing each other after the last court battle and move on?"

Again he thought a moment. "I suppose so." He checked his watch. "Let's catch some television and forget about this for the moment. We'll watch the news at eleven and see what kind of trouble we really have before we get too hysterical."

The mood was tense, and Hugh didn't even think to steal a kiss while Mrs. Simms was out of the room.

Kendra pet Hamlette occasionally, still impressed that she was now trained well enough to stay inside. She fidgeted impatiently, wondering what the press would do to their reputations.

Hugh must be eager to know what will happen to him.

As if reading her mind, he said, "Don't worry." He kissed the top of her head. "They can't do anything to us except embarrass us."

If only he'd been right.

When the news came on, Kendra tensed and could feel Hugh do the same.

The anchorman stared at the camera without expression. "In tonight's top stories . . ." Kendra held her breath. ". . . Assistant District Attorney Hugh Cramer is being investigated for fixing cases."

They both gasped. Kendra's hand flew to her mouth. *Oh, no.*

A few moments later the scene moved to their kiss in the arena's parking lot. Vickie Sawyer's voice gave the picture its own story. "As you can see, ADA Hugh Cramer may be guilty of ethics violations. Evidently he has been involved with a woman he recently 'pretended' to prosecute. Kendra Simms, as you'll recall, was last in court on charges of assaulting a police officer. Here she is seen in the arms of the prosecuting attorney. She's been in and out of court for the last few years on charges ranging from disturbing the peace to this last one, assault. Mr. Cramer has lost cases against her in the past. Being a qualified and, from what this reporter can find, capable lawyer, one must wonder why he can't seem to successfully prosecute one person. We may now have our answer. Back to you, Sam."

Sam took over where Vickie left off. "In the studio with us we have Police Chief Marvin Cary."

"Thanks for having me, Sam." The men shook hands across the console. "When Miss Sawyer called, I had to come here in person to tell you how this situation reflects on our community. I have called the president of the board of directors of Miss Simms' shelter and asked to be heard on this. Also, I have spoken with District Attorney Walter Henry. He and I will meet tomorrow. I want this taken care of immediately. Mr. Cramer and Miss Simms are acting in a totally inappropriate manner, and I want to make sure that this failure to convict Miss Simms of her many crimes against this community is not because she's been dating her prosecutor all along."

Hugh grabbed a cork coaster from the end table and threw it at the television. It bounced off harmlessly. "Do you see this? In one fell swoop Sawyer and Cary are killing my career and yours with it."

Her stomach in knots, Kendra couldn't speak.

"Cary will close your shelter, Kendra. Make no mistake about it. He'll close it, and I'll lose everything I've worked for too." Denunciations rolled off his tongue, relegating both the chief and Vickie Sawyer to a hot eternity.

"We can fight this, Hugh. There's no sense in losing our sanity over it."

"You'll probably be okay. You've gotten some bad press before, Kendra. But my career? Just the *suggestion* that I might be losing cases on purpose could ruin me."

"Try not to worry too much. I'm sure there's something we can do."

"I'm going. I'll call you."

His words held a finality she didn't want to face. "Is that it? You're just walking away with your tail tucked between your legs?" she challenged him.

The phone rang as he asked, "What would you have me do, Kendra?"

She picked it up and found the president of her board of directors.

"Kendra, Harold Frey here. We need to speak to you as soon as possible. I'm getting the board together for a lunch meeting at the Village Restaurant. I hope you'll join us at twelve-thirty tomorrow."

"Mr. Frey, if this is about the news tonight—"

"And, Kendra, please don't be late."

Unlike anything he had ever done before, Harold Frey not only ordered her to do something, he hung up on her before she could explain, complain, or even say good-bye.

Hugh wasn't the only one in trouble.

He'd stood by as she took her call. "What was that?"

She put the phone back onto the receiver. "The board is meeting tomorrow. I'm to be at the Village Restaurant at half past twelve. It seems your job isn't the only one at risk."

When Hugh got to work, he found Lydia in tears. "I'm to tell you not to go to your office. You are to go straight to the conference room. I'm sorry, Hugh. I know you'd never do anything wrong."

The fallout.

When he entered the room, Walter Henry and Chief Cary sat at the table.

Hugh placed his briefcase on the table. "I assume you caught the eleven o'clock news?"

Cary's face was set in a vicious expression.

"I not only saw it, I got to be a part of it. You and your little girlfriend are going to rue the day you crossed me."

Hugh sat down across from the chief and eyed him until the man's evil smile faded. "All you're worried about is your new property's value."

Walter Henry threw a piece of paper in front of Hugh. "Read this."

Hugh gave it a cursory glance. "This is notification that I'm under investigation by the White County DA's office. *Your* office."

Henry glared. "That's what I have been advised to do. You lost your cases against Miss Simms, and we need to know if it's because you were romantically involved with her."

Hugh shifted in his chair. "This can be straightened out in a simple interview."

Walter glanced at Cary and returned his gaze to Hugh. "I think we're thinking about a deposition, not an interview."

Cary jumped into the fray. "I really don't care what you and Miss Simms did or didn't do. I want that shelter gone. Without it, my property value jumps at least twenty-five thousand dollars. You have her close that shelter, and I'll withdraw my complaints, and you can go back to business as usual . . . whatever that business is."

Hugh stood and put the document he held onto the table. After a deep breath, he slammed his fist on top of it. The other men jumped.

"Business as usual? All you want from me is to pressure Kendra Simms to close her shelter. Is that what you said? You don't care about the fact that she's devoted her entire adult life to saving helpless animals. All that matters to you is money!"

Neither spoke.

Hugh continued his tirade, directing it full force on his boss. "And you, Walter. You are every reason attorneys have a bad reputation. You are so worried about politics, you're no good as a prosecutor. I told you from the beginning that Kendra wasn't a menace to society, but no. You had to listen to this pigheaded, overblown—"

Cary jumped from his chair. "You'd better be careful there, Mr. Cramer."

"Or what? You going to have someone ticket my car? If I were you, I'd find myself an attorney who is just as manipulative as you are. The one thing you both forgot is that I love the law, and I sure as hell know how to make it work for the innocent."

Hugh stormed from the room and into his office. Lydia wasn't at her desk. He'd call her later. He grabbed the few personal items he had in the undersized room and put them into his briefcase before he left.

When he walked out the door, he knew it wasn't for the last time. Just the last time as an ADA.

Chapter Ten

Kendra dreaded this meeting to the point that she almost became ill before going into it.

Harold Frey welcomed her, however coolly, into the private room at the restaurant.

There was no time for small talk, and she saw something she hadn't expected. Pete Randall sat quietly in the back of the room. He was back. With graveness in his dark eyes, he nodded.

"Kendra, there is no reason to keep you in suspense as to why this meeting was called. Mrs. Wellington of the Clinton Heights Community Organization phoned me and asked the board to remove you from the leadership of the Rescue."

Her worst fear realized, Kendra's heart fell into her shoes.

"Before you panic, though, we want you to tell us the truth."

Someone else called out, "Kendra, you've never lied to us before. We'll believe you now. Just tell us."

Pete Randall nodded as he lifted a small video camera to his shoulder. The words weren't spoken, but she could almost hear him say, *Here's your chance, sweetie. Clear your name for me again.*

"All right." She didn't sit down at a table, but she did ask for a glass of water and sipped some before she spoke. "During that last ridiculous lawsuit, I found myself attracted to Hugh Cramer. But we didn't date until it was settled. Since then we have seen each other on occasion."

Pete yelled from his seat, "Miss Simms! Is that all there is to this?"

"Yes." The tears stung her eyes, but she refused to shed them on television.

"Who do you think is behind your current problems with the press?"

"I won't name anyone in particular. But I will say two things. I can't seem to take a breath without finding the lead reporter from

Channel Seven watching me. I feel as if I'm being stalked. The other thing is that, with the animal shelter gone, the property values in Clinton Heights would go up dramatically. Many residents there are politically influential, Mr. Randall. You do the math."

Mr. Frey's gaze darted about the room. "I'm sorry, my dear, but until this matter is resolved, we must ask you to take an administrative leave."

That broke her. She left the room in a rush of tears. She knew Pete would do what he could to help her; he always did. But losing her position at the Rescue, even if only for a short time, hurt her in a way she couldn't put into words.

At home, Kendra tried to pull herself together before her mother returned from her gardening club. Joan had been at the Rescue when she stopped there to pick up some personal items. She wasn't sure which one of them had cried the hardest.

Kendra retreated to her basement apartment and turned on the television. When she heard her mother come into the house, she didn't go upstairs to greet her. She didn't want to face her right now.

She lay on her bed, tossing and turning, and

finally dozed fitfully. Nightmares plagued her nap.

Near six o'clock she woke and wandered up to the living room. Her mother took one look at her and asked her what had happened.

She turned the channel to the news.

Channel Seven used her misfortune as the top story, complete with the tale of Hugh's resignation from the District Attorney's office and her forced administrative leave from the shelter. Vickie Sawyer did her usual best at making a case against Kendra. Hugh, of course, stood in the worst fallout. He'd had to resign!

Pete Randall, much kinder in his presentation, made the story his third of the night, showing the film he'd taken of her at the lunch meeting.

She'd thank him for that the next time she saw him.

Perhaps the worst part of the day was that she'd heard nothing from Hugh. He'd disappeared. When a knock came at the door, she fully expected it to be him. However, when she opened the door, a man she didn't know shoved a piece of paper at her. Caught by surprise, she took it.

"Kendra J. Simms, consider yourself served with a subpoena from the District Attorney's office."

"What?"

The man moved down the steps and down the walk. "Just read it, ma'am."

The phone rang then, and when her mother answered it, she handed it to Kendra.

"Hello?"

"Hey, hon. It's me."

Relief coursed through her. It was him. *The rat. Why didn't he call sooner?*

"I'm sorry I didn't call you earlier. I was so tied up in my situation, I didn't even realize you were in trouble until the news came on. Are you okay?"

"No. I'm not okay, Hugh. My Rescue is going to be taken away. Now that Cary has me out of there, he'll find a way to close it. Just wait."

"I'm sure you're right. That's why I'm try-ing to move fast."

While she'd pined away all afternoon, Hugh had worked to salvage the Rescue.

"Danni or Michael can help you with any legal needs you have."

"What about you?"

"I can't because of the circumstances."

"That's not what I meant. I'm standing here holding some kind of subpoena."

"I was afraid of that. Kendra, I'm under investigation right now. Cary and Walter Henry will probably drag us both through the mud. I'm so sorry. I should have protected you from this."

"Protect *me?* That's a hoot."

"A hoot?" he echoed softly.

"Hugh, you're a great attorney, but I've dealt with this stuff on my own before." Her own words encouraged her as she spoke them. Her misery was replaced by her usual fighting spirit.

"I see," he replied quietly.

Already she felt more like the person who had taken on Chief Cary and Mrs. Wellington in the Clinton Heights community center that evening a couple of months ago.

Hugh, however, sounded different. Almost remote. "Then I'll get back to work on my situation. Would you let me see your subpoena?"

"Oh!" With her newfound courage, she'd almost forgotten it. "Yes. Sure. When?"

"Tomorrow. Meet me in Mike Sommars' office at ten. If you can, of course."

She chuckled. "It appears my schedule is free and clear."

"I'll see you then." He rang off without another word. No gentleness. No reassurances.
Had she missed something?

Did he blame her? He'd had to quit his job,
after all. What a blow.

That night, she tossed and turned until day-
break. As strong as she wanted to be, the truth
was, she was scared. Not only of losing Hugh,
but of losing the Rescue as well.

As she showered and got dressed the next
morning, it occurred to her that she'd never
really had Hugh anyway.

It wasn't as if they'd had a normal courtship.
Out-of-town movies and dining. All exciting
at first, she admitted to herself, but the truth
was, she was tired of it and sometimes wanted
to say, "Look at me! I'm on a date with this
great guy!"

Not that anyone, she thought as she drove
herself to Michael's office, really said that
kind of thing, but it would have been nice if,
for example, she'd had the chance to meet
Hugh's mother.

She never liked being kept waiting, but
Kendra found herself enduring just that in the
lobby at Cole, Sommars and Sommars.

Hugh strode through the doorway and went
straight to the receptionist's desk. They spoke

in low tones for a moment; then the young woman pointed toward Kendra.

Hugh faced her. It was the first time they'd seen each other since they'd watched the newscast together.

His aloof manner didn't help. "Kendra. It's good to see you. Did you bring the subpoena?"

She handed him the document. "I read over it. I think you're in much worse trouble than I am," she fretted.

"Not really. You may lose your Rescue." He perused the paper as he spoke. "I know how important that is to you."

A door opened, and Michael Sommars emerged. "Hugh, Kendra, come on in. Let's see what we can do for you guys."

Hugh's coolness led Kendra to suspect she didn't even need to be there. She waved at Michael. "I don't think so, Michael. I'll go my usual route on this."

Michael disagreed with her plan. "Better not. You don't have just yourself to think about. The entire shelter could be at risk if you don't seek proper representation."

Kendra stood her ground. "I've been through this kind of stupidity before."

"Not like this." His cobalt blue eyes full of sadness, he explained, "You're in the middle of a war over the land where the shelter sits. Cary said if the Rescue was closed, he could make sure all this trouble went away."

Anger flashed through her. "Is that your plan?" she asked Hugh.

"If that were my plan, do you think I'd be standing here? I'd be better off asking Santa for an elephant than asking you to give up the shelter. But you'll have to do it if he wins this thing." His eyes searched her face. "That's what you need to think about."

For a moment she pictured just that. What would she do if the shelter closed? What about all the animals? "I . . ." She looked at Michael. "I don't have the money to pay you."

"I'm not interested in the money." His handsome smile had a touch of mischievousness to it. "I'm interested in seeing a few corrupt politicians get what they deserve."

Kendra faltered. She could take the route she normally did and try to spin the media to help her cause. However, with the news what it was at this point, did she really want to take that chance?

And *chance* would be the word. If she failed at her game, she'd lose the Rescue. Worse than that, the animals would lose everything.

What could she do but go along with whatever plan Michael Sommars concocted? She didn't have the money, or the nerve, to do anything else.

A sigh escaped her lips. "Okay. I'll listen to what you have to say. I won't promise that I'll go along with you." *But I will. Unless my fairy godmother comes around.*

Inside Michael's office she and Hugh sat in soft leather chairs opposite Mike, who positioned himself behind the large oak desk. As much trouble as she had been in before, she'd never really had to hire a criminal attorney or think much about politics.

She realized what was bothering her. Fear. When she'd been in trouble in the past, it was mostly just hoopla caused by a demonstration or two.

She'd never been really afraid until now.

The shelter was in real trouble. The Rescue she'd devoted her heart and soul to could be closed, all because she chose to kiss the wrong man at the wrong time.

Even worse, she knew that Hugh wasn't the wrong man. He was the right one, but right now he was so distant and different than he'd been before.

Had politics taken over the sweet, gentle man she'd come to care for so deeply?

"If you're thinking you can walk out of here

and handle the press the way you usually do, forget it, Kendra," Michael summarized. "This is going to get really nasty. More so than anything you've seen before."

"What would you do?" she asked him.

"I'd let me handle the leave the shelter gave you, and in the meantime . . ." He paused and took a deep breath. "You might want to think about a job change."

Kendra's stomach flipped. "Michael, I . . ."

"You've been *the* spokesperson in this town for animal rights, but now people might be seeing you as someone who's been making loopholes in the law."

Hugh nodded. "And, Kendra, they think we've been doing something illegal all along."

"I'm not going to let a few reporters ruin my life, guys. You shouldn't either."

"You don't get it! I'm under investigation by the District Attorney's office. They're just waiting to get enough on me to also bring charges against you."

"They wouldn't dare."

Michael put his pencil on the desk. "Don't believe that for a minute. They would not only dare, they'd love it. If they can ruin your image, regardless of the truth, they can close the shelter too."

She wouldn't allow that to happen. "So we play the media."

Hugh got up as he spoke, frustration written all over him. "This isn't your usual game. It's too big for that!"

She jumped from her chair to stand face-to-face with him. "Why? Because I don't have a law degree? I can fight this, and you could too, if you had the nerve!"

"This isn't *about* nerve."

"It's about fear. You're both so afraid of Cary and Henry that you can't see the forest for the trees. This is our chance to prove what's really going on around here. You can show what Walter Henry is really doing as District Attorney. You can make it clear he's a politician, not a prosecutor."

Hugh sighed. "Is that supposed to be a news flash? Most DAs *are* politicians first, prosecutors second. It's the nature of the beast."

She huffed, "Fine! But if we can show how he's abusing that power to put us in such a precarious position—"

"Right now you look like a woman who's living in a glass house, not like someone who can point a finger at public officials who might be bending the laws to suit their purposes."

She took a step back from him. "Is that how *you* see me?"

"Of course not!"

"You see me as the woman who's single-handedly ruining your career."

"I see you as a part of this situation—I won't lie about that."

"And this 'situation' is something you want to be rid of, right?"

He rolled his eyes.

Michael finally stood. "Kids! Kids! It's time to calm down and work. If you two can't pull it together, you could actually end up in jail."

Kendra's eyes implored Michael. "What're the odds of that?"

"It's the worst-case scenario, but it could happen."

Hugh tempered his anger. "You don't have to scare her like that."

"Do you think I said that to scare her? She—and you, for that matter—could see the inside of a cell if this isn't settled. Neither one of you can afford a misstep right now. I thought that's why you came here, Hugh. I assumed you recognized the seriousness of what's happening."

Hugh nodded, and a silence settled over the threesome.

Kendra realized that any people outside Mike's door had probably heard every word she and Hugh exchanged. Her entire face heated at the thought. What must they think? She was at one of the most prestigious law firms in town, yelling like some banshee at the man.

"Now"—Michael walked to the door—"if you'll excuse us, Kendra, I'm going to talk to Hugh in private. Then you'll have your turn. I need to get a better handle on what this is all about. It's obvious you're upset, as well you should be. But we need calm heads right now."

Kendra went to a park down the street from the office. It was a pretty place in the middle of downtown, where many people took a bagged lunch and ate at wrought iron tables surrounded by a few dogwoods and greenery.

Allowing the cool breeze to surround her, she picked a bench to sit on and contemplate her situation.

No matter how she viewed it, she'd lost the Rescue.

She'd lost Hugh.

Heck, she'd even lost her reputation. How had all that happened? Vickie Sawyer jumped into her mind. Everything she wanted hinged on how she could fight the woman.

And win.

Hmm. Her thoughts wandered into dangerous territory, but, heck, dangerous territory was her home away from home.

Chapter Eleven

Pete Randall wasn't the nicest guy in the world, granted. But for whatever reason, he liked Kendra and always played up the Rescue as good for Fort White.

That was a friend, no matter how you cut it.

At least that's what she hoped as she entered his office.

The words STATION MANAGER beamed at her from the door.

Pete kissed her on the cheek and told her to have a seat. "Glad you came by."

"Thanks for seeing me."

He lit a cigar. "So, little girl, why do you darken this old man's door?"

"I need help."

"You're telling me? You and ADA Hugh Cramer are the talk of the town. What exactly did you do?"

"I'm not guilty of any crime. Neither is Mr. Cramer. We're just victims of some bad press."

"Yeah. Vickie Sawyer took a dislike to you ages ago."

"Yeah, and she's a control freak. One who wants the world at her feet."

He nodded. "She's a diva. I'll give you that."

Kendra sat forward in her chair. "Pete, as far as I can see, no one has been appointed as interim director over at the Rescue. I'm afraid Cary will close it. Please help me stop him."

"Do you have any ideas?"

"That's where I hoped for your help. Michael Sommars said he'll act as my legal counsel."

"You can't do much better than that, even if I don't like the guy."

"What's that all about?"

"His father made my second divorce a nightmare. Fortunately for me, my ex lost support if she remarried, and she did that pretty quickly."

"My question is, are you going to help me?"

He sat back in his chair. "I have to focus on what's best for the station, Kendra. You know I think the world of you, but—"

Although he'd stopped in midsentence, apparently Kendra wasn't the reason. For a moment he went glassy-eyed, his thoughts elsewhere.

Next he jumped from his chair, startling her. He opened the door of his office and yelled, "Miller! Get in here, and bring Peters with you!" Then he gave Kendra a sly smile. "I am a genius. I think I know how I can save your Rescue, and possibly even you with it."

She hugged him. "You're my knight in shining armor."

"Let's be honest—it's a little rusty. But it'll get the job done."

Hugh lay on top of the blankets on his bed, reviewing law books. He tried to find precedents for his situation, but they weren't exactly in great numbers.

He slammed the heavy tome shut.

"If only I'd been more cautious." He shook his head, as if anyone were there to see it.

Everything that was important to him was about an inch away from being destroyed.

He had no relationship with Kendra now.

His career was in tatters.

He might even come out of this mess with a criminal record.

When the phone rang, he didn't bother to

check the caller ID, because things couldn't get any worse. "Hello?"

"Curtis Hugh Cramer," he heard.

Things couldn't get any worse, huh? Obviously he'd spoken too soon. "Hi, Mom."

"What on earth is going on? Your job is in jeopardy. You're all over the news. What happened?"

"Mom, it's all a misunderstanding. Nothing to worry about. I promise," he reassured her.

"Who is this girl they keep showing you with? What kind of person can she be if you never mentioned her to me? And what happened to that nice Celia Blake I introduced you to?"

"Mom, Kendra Simms is a really nice person. You're going to like her much better than Celia."

"Not if she's the reason you lose your job and throw your career away. Your dad must be rolling over in his grave."

"I doubt that. He'd probably be happy that I'm in love."

"If she's such a nice girl, why haven't we been introduced?"

"Mom, I don't want to talk about this right now."

"Okay, you name the time."

He drew a deep breath. "Okay, this is what

happened. I fell in love with this beautiful girl, but she had stabbed a cop with a carrot, and I had to prosecute her."

A long silence met his ears.

"Mom?"

"Did you say she stabbed a police officer with a carrot?"

"Yes."

"A carrot, as in salad-with-ranch-dressing carrot?"

"That's what I'm talking about."

Her tone changed to one of disbelief. "You took her to court for using a carrot to stab someone. Was he hurt?"

It took over an hour to calm his mother and explain the real situation. When he finished, she understood his position and even tried to think of ways to help him.

None of which did.

"The best thing you can do for me right now is to offer me a good home-cooked meal someday soon and to believe in me."

"I believe in you, honey. I always have. And I hope you will come for dinner very soon."

When they rang off, Hugh felt a small sense of relief. If his mom still believed in him, there was no reason for him not to think he could fix this and come out smelling like a rose.

He picked up the phone and dialed Kendra.

When her mother answered and told him she was with a television person trying to fix all her bad publicity, he thanked her and hung up.

But after leaping from the bed, he stalked around his apartment, finding shoes and decent clothing while anger poured through him like molten lava.

He'd set Kendra straight once and for all.

She needed to let Michael Sommars settle this for them, but she was already out trying to escalate all the problems they already had.

When he found her, he'd strangle her. He'd do whatever it took to keep her from making this worse than it was.

He slammed the door to his sedan and started it, considering where he would find her.

The answer was obvious.

Who'd kissed her that night at the Clinton Heights gig? He'd find her in the arms of one Pete Randall.

He'd kill them both when he did.

Pete had a great idea.

He decided it was timely to do a thirty-minute special on the Seaton Animal Rescue. He'd not only talk about Kendra's work throughout the show, but he'd showcase the animals, the no-kill policy, the pets they'd placed, the pet therapy, the works.

Unfortunately, it could take weeks to put together. Another problem would be convincing programming and sales that the special would still be a marketable item by then. Being station manager, Kendra discovered, didn't necessarily mean Pete had the last say on everything.

Losing her job didn't matter to her so much anymore. She'd just go to the unemployment office and worry later about her career. The Rescue's survival was first and foremost in her mind.

As she exited the television station, Hugh drove up in his late-model sedan, parked right in front of her—illegally—and jumped out to stand in front of her. Fury radiated from him. "What do you think you're doing?"

"I'm trying to save the Rescue."

"Save it? Didn't you hear Mike? You won't save the Rescue with more publicity, Kendra. You do as your attorney tells you, and stay away from the media."

"Pete is my friend."

"I believe you. I even believe he would avoid hurting you or the Rescue. What I don't believe is that you know what you're doing right now."

"What does that mean? That I'm stupid?"

"It means you haven't dealt with something this big before. This time you weren't accused of just stabbing someone with a carrot. You're in trouble. Big trouble. Someone should put you on a leash, the way you're acting."

"I resent that, Hugh. I know what I'm doing. I've played the media for years, and I'm pretty damn good at it. Maybe you could use some advice from me on this. After all, it's the media that started it."

"Tell me about it. Your shadow, Sawyer, has me signed, sealed, and delivered to the dump." He sighed. "I have to go. Need a lift?"

"I've got my car, but let's take a ride."

She got into his car. He maneuvered away from the station and parked in the mall parking lot, far away from other cars.

"I'm in deep trouble too, Kendra," he admitted. He turned the car off. "Colleagues shun me. People who've known me for years won't take my calls. I heard they might even ask the state Attorney General to send a task force to investigate every case I've worked on, even before I came to the DA's office."

"Oh, Hugh, I'm so sorry."

"Marvin Cary is doing all he can to make this situation as bad as possible. He really wants that shelter gone."

"Then tell people that. Tell them what he's doing. Don't just sit there and take it."

He started the car and pulled out. "You don't get it. No one will listen to me. No one."

"Michael's listening. I'm sure Danni is too. What about the judge?"

"The judge won't take my calls. Michael is my legal counsel. Danni is my friend. That's practically all I have right now, except my own mother." He pulled up next to her SUV back at the television station.

"I'm here, Hugh. Where I've always been."

His voice held a note of sadness. "Thanks. But right now we can't really afford to be seen together."

Her heart fell as she got out of the car and walked to her own.

He blames me.

And well he should.

Chapter Twelve

"If you're not going to eat those, I'll take them." Alex Price reached across the table and grabbed some fries from Hugh's plate. "You're missing a great meal by pouting."

Hugh snorted. "You call this pouting? I could show you some real pouting—if you weren't so busy eating my lunch."

"I got a call from Pete Randall. The one who runs a television station. He's doing some kind of special report on the Seaton Animal Rescue to try to keep it up and running while your friend Kendra Simms isn't there. I gave him an interview. I wish I could help more."

"Did you talk about using the animals for pet therapy at your clinic?"

"Yup. I told them how pet therapy helps our patients and about how Kendra's animals find good homes. As far as I'm concerned, it's a win-win situation."

Hugh applauded the performance. "You *are* good. I hope you did that well in front of the cameras."

Smiling, Alex grabbed more fries. "You liked that, huh? That's the spiel I gave them. I hope it works. I hear that a couple of volunteers are trying to keep things going at the shelter, but it doesn't look good."

"The Clinton Heights residents might just get what they want."

"That doesn't seem right."

Hugh picked up his soda and sipped it through the straw. "No, it certainly doesn't."

"Forget the Rescue for now. What about you and Kendra?"

"I think when she sees me, all she thinks about is losing her first love. That shelter is everything to her. Has been for years. And what am I doing? Getting her and it into more and more trouble. Truth is, I don't think she'll ever forgive me." He poked the straw farther into the drink.

"But you don't really know any of this for sure?"

He didn't answer.

"You're guessing. You have no idea how she really feels. You're too scared to ask her, right?"

"It's hard to hear a woman you care about say she doesn't want anything to do with you. Although, with your track record, I shouldn't have to tell you that."

"Ha-ha. We're funny today, aren't we? As brokenhearted as you're supposed to be, you shouldn't be cracking jokes. In fact, all jokes should be left to the experts."

"And that would be you?"

"Absolutely. You know, you could always go with me to get Hamlette the pig. I told Danni I'd pick her up on my way to Mom's. She wants her to spend time with Joey." He grunted. "Do you believe that? The pig needs piggy company!"

"I'll go. Sounds like a chance for you to see us together. You can see for yourself the way she acts."

Alex nodded.

The time with Alex afforded Hugh a break from his miserable life. Danni's brother could make anything a joke, and he was in rare form today, even for him. Nothing they talked about as they drove to Kendra's remained serious; they both avoided discussing anything significant.

The mood, however, broke immediately upon their arrival at Kendra's house, where a police car was parked, red lights flashing.

A policeman stood on her porch, yelling, "I'm telling you ma'am, I want that pig! I have a warrant for him!"

Inside the screen door, Kendra answered exactly as Hugh would have expected.

"You don't even know she's a girl! You aren't getting her! You'll have to arrest me!"

"What's going on?" Hugh slammed the door after getting out of the car.

The policeman looked relieved to see someone else come onto the scene. "We have a warrant to return the pig"—he read from the form in his hand—"known as Hamlette, to the Seaton Animal Rescue."

"Let me see that, please."

The officer hesitated.

"I'm acting as Miss Simms' attorney," he fibbed.

The cop gave him the paper. Hugh read it and became angry in seconds. "These people haven't done enough? They want to rob her of the pig as well?"

The officer answered, "I just do what I'm told on these warrants, sir. All I know is what you see in this document."

Kendra's expression told him she was ready for a fight, but she didn't speak.

"I'll take responsibility for the pig." It was Alex who spoke.

"I'm sorry." The policeman obviously didn't like the situation; he seemed a little embarrassed. "We have to take the pig and return it to the shelter. After that, you can probably adopt it."

Kendra started to speak, but Hugh didn't let her. "Let Hamlette go. Alex and I will go get her and bring her back to you."

"I can fight this."

"And as good as you are, you could even win, Kendra. But with all that's happening around us right now, the less publicity, the better."

It was then that the news crew from Channel Seven pulled up in front of Kendra's already crowded house.

"What a nightmare."

Her murmured words reached his ears, and Hugh turned to see what Kendra saw.

The expletive that escaped his lips startled Kendra, but she couldn't help but agree with it.

"This stops here." She marched out the door and toward Vickie Sawyer, who was exiting the van. "Miss Sawyer."

"Miss Simms. Seems as if you and I can't help but keep running into each other."

Her smug grin almost provoked Kendra to become physical.

Total control freak, she reminded herself.

"Could you tell me why you're here?" she asked politely.

"To report the news, of course."

"And can you tell me to what news you're referring?"

"We are here in response to a call that you were being forced to return an animal you stole from the shelter. We wanted to know—"

"May I ask who called you?"

"I don't reveal my—"

"Can you tell me why you hound me like a dog with a bone? Can you also explain to the good people of Fort White why you don't give them any real news? Can you tell us all who's paying you to disrupt my life on an almost daily basis? I believe 'inquiring minds' would like to know. I know I would. You won't leave me alone, yet the other news venues in this city aren't all over me, and they get the more truthful views of—"

Vickie pushed a microphone into Kendra's face. She had to realize she'd lost control of the situation, and she was desperate to get it back. "Can you tell us why you stole an animal from the shelter?"

"Can you tell me who told you such a slanderous thing? I'd like to sue."

"Are you sure you can do that, with your criminal past and all?"

"The only 'past' I have is the one you've made up. You're a horrible person, Miss Sawyer. I feel sorry for you, because eventually what goes around comes around."

Kendra trekked back into her house. Hugh had stepped inside, away from the cameras. Alex followed Kendra in and told her he'd go to the shelter and get Hamlette for her and take her to Danni's as they'd planned.

It wasn't like Kendra, but this time she broke down. Flopping onto the couch, she let the tears flow. Hugh sat down next to her and held her.

"Are they gone?" she asked through her sobs.

He gently set her away from him and strode to the window. Carefully he pushed the curtain a fraction of an inch to see out. "I think so. Though it really won't help to be caught peeping out the window."

"This whole ridiculous situation will be the death of me if something doesn't happen soon."

Hugh only nodded in agreement.

"Hugh, I'm finished. I don't know if I could even find another job in this town."

"I can hang out a shingle anywhere, so even if this goes sour for me at the DA's office, I can probably still work. Unless . . ."

"Unless what?"

"Unless we lose. If we do, I could do jail time and lose my license."

Kendra was nearly hysterical. "Do you really think we'll go to jail?"

"I don't think so, but even if we lost and got probation, my career would be over."

Kendra picked up the phone. "I can be a victim for only so long."

A few moments later she spoke again. "Mr. Frey, this is Kendra Simms. I want to know why you got a warrant to take Hamlette."

"Kendra, dear—"

"Enough of the 'Kendra dear' talk. I want to know why you did it. And when you're finished explaining that, I want to know why the Channel Seven news crew was here to video the whole thing."

"Are you insinuating that I called the media?"

"No, sir, I am not. I'm telling you straight out that unless the board wants to get sued, you'll meet with me and my attorney tonight.

I will no longer sit here in my house and worry about you people. You were all brought on board by me, not the other way around. I've given my life to the Rescue. Can you say the same?"

"I will not be talked to in this manner."

"Fine, then you can talk to Michael Sommars. He'll take care of you and whatever connection you have to the media."

"I didn't call the press. Chief Cary must have. He was the one who told us to get the warrant for the pig."

"And you just bow down and do whatever he tells you to do? When did this start?"

"We're afraid of what you've done, Kendra. You've gotten yourself into lots of trouble this time. This Assistant DA you've been carrying on with—"

"I haven't been 'carrying on.' I was involved with a nice guy. There's nothing in my contract about not dating."

"No. But there is a clause regarding ethics. If you were involved while you were on trial, then you will lose your job."

"And if I wasn't?"

"We'll see."

"No, you won't. When I'm exonerated, I will be reinstated, or you can count on a lawsuit."

"I won't make any promises."

"Who's running the shelter now?"

"Joan. She's doing a fine job. We aren't taking any more animals, and she's finding homes for the ones we do have."

"Why aren't we taking any more?"

"That doesn't have anything to do with you at this point, does it?"

"You just made a very big mistake."

She hung up without saying good-bye. Anger boiled in her. "They're making plans to close the shelter," she said bitterly.

Hugh stood from where he'd sat in an overstuffed chair. "He said that?"

"Not in so many words."

"What's the plan?"

"I'll do the logical thing and go see Michael. But unless he can come up with a good reason not to, you're about to see me go into battle mode."

"I don't know. . . ." He took her hand in his, then grinned at her. "Maybe battle mode is what we need after all."

"Hugh, you mean a lot to me. You know that, right?"

"I'd hoped."

"We might have to fight this alone, each in our own way. If we do, that doesn't mean I don't care. I want you to know that. But you also need to understand that I don't play the martyr well. I'm going to sit at this table and lay out a plan, and you might not agree with it, but I'm going to get my shelter back."

"Then I'd better hang around to keep the plan legal."

"Or leave, so you don't get into trouble if it's not."

Chapter Thirteen

Alex called and said there was a problem. Hugh took it on his cell phone and didn't know how in the world he could put this on Kendra after everything else they were already going through. When he hung up, she glanced up from the kitchen table, where they had notepads in front of them.

She picked up her drink and asked, "Was that Alex?"

"Yeah. It seems that Hamlette has already been adopted."

She slammed her glass down. "Adopted? By whom?"

"Chief Cary."

"The man himself. Well, that's just the per-fect ending to a perfect day, isn't it, Hugh?"

She picked up her phone and dialed a num-ber. "Hey, girl! I need some backup. You wanna go start a riot? Great! Tonight okay with you? Good! I'll call you back in about an hour. Oh, we're going to picket in front of Chief Cary's house. He stole my pig."

Hugh didn't even wait for her to hang up. "You wouldn't!"

Her head bobbed a positive response, and her grin was as mischievous as that of a little kid getting ready to open a Christmas present found in the back of a closet.

He used his cell to call Michael, but Som-mars was in court.

When she hung up, Hugh begged Kendra, "Don't do this."

"All of this doing it your way is over. If I'm found guilty of something, then I am. But I'm going to play the game I know."

"Fine. The game you know, however, could bury both of us. I can't stand with you on this, Kendra. If I do, they'll have proven their point about us."

"Is that how you see it?"

"That's how anyone and everyone will see it. And if I get arrested with you, I'll be thrown out of the Bar Association. Everything I've worked for all my life will be over."

"It's the same for me, Hugh. But I'm tired of mourning. I'm going for the victory. You have to choose what you'll do."

"I know. I'm sorry, Kendra. I'm going home."

Her heart fell. "I understand. We each have to do what we think is right." She grabbed her purse. "If you want a ride, I'll take you home."

"You can drop me off at Danni's."

The group of people was formed by friends calling friends calling friends. Kendra knew a lot about putting together a demonstration. She'd been doing it since she was twenty-one.

"The Seaton Animal Rescue is in trouble." Pete Randall had once more come to Kendra's aid. "The director has been accused of something a little more serious this time than stabbing a policeman with a carrot. I'm here with Kendra Simms, and she is willing to talk with me about what is happening around us."

"Thanks for coming, Pete. It appears that Chief Cary has made it his personal vendetta to destroy the Rescue and me with it. In fact, he doesn't seem to care which one of us goes first."

"Miss Simms, can you tell me exactly why we are here in front Chief Cary's house, what the 'Let Hamlette Go' signs are all about, and why you put this demonstration together?"

"The potbellied pig that one of my neighbors tried to kill and I saved was staying with me. I was told by Harold Frey, the president of the board of directors of the Rescue, that at the chief's urging, he got a warrant for her return to the shelter. Then, afterward, I found out the chief had 'adopted' her."

"Why would he adopt her?"

"That's a very good question. I hope he'll come outside to tell me. But I doubt that he will. People like him tend to bully from afar."

"What about the charges that you and ADA Hugh Cramer have been seeing each other for quite a long time, and that is why you've won all your cases?"

"It's a fabrication, and I believe, the chief might be involved in that also. However, let me make something perfectly clear. Hugh Cramer became a friend of mine after my last trial. But we were not involved before then. Also, I was accused of assaulting a man with a carrot. Judge Cole himself threw the case out of court. Ask him why he did it. There is no one on the bench more honorable. Do you honestly think he'd ruin his record over whom I might or might not be dating?"

Pete tried to hide a chuckle. "Okay, and who are all these people with you tonight?"

"These are people who understand that the chief and others bought prime real estate next door to the Rescue and now want to be rid of the 'nuisance.' But the shelter was here first, and we all believe we should try to live together instead of ruining the shelter, which does such wonderful work for this community."

That piece aired at 6:00. By 8:00 the group had grown from sixty people to at least two hundred.

Perhaps that was why it wasn't such a good idea for the chief to decide he should make an appearance. The crowd became tense, and Kendra worried she'd bitten off more than she could chew.

Pete now set his mic so it would feed to the TV station and also act as an amplifier.

He ushered the chief to his news van, and Kendra joined them. She asked for order, and, surprisingly, the crowd did quiet down.

Kendra peered over the audience and spotted Hugh. His arms were crossed, and a smile of admiration lit his handsome face.

He came!

The chief read a prepared speech to the audience. "I have been painted as a bad public servant in this picture, but I assure you it isn't true. Don't believe everything a woman like Kendra Simms—a woman who is desperate to save her job—says. Everyone knows her record. She can't stay out of court, and she has a reason she isn't in jail. I believe we all know what it is."

He ended his speech by saying, "The little pig she keeps referring to is feral. It should be put down, and I will do my duty as your police chief and assure you that that will happen—"

Not a good thing to say at that moment. The crowd chanted "Save Hamlette!" They'd lost their patience with the enemy.

Kendra grabbed Pete's mic and again asked for quiet. She was the only one who could calm the crowd.

Hugh stepped forward and took the mic the chief had used. "Excuse me, Chief Cary?"

The older man twisted around, glaring at Hugh.

"If you'll do me the honor, I'd like to question you about this situation. There may be no need to ruin two people's lives because of a property dispute."

Hugh knew the chief well enough to know he wouldn't walk away without getting in the last word. He banked on it. His blood pumped harder as the chief turned back to comply.

"You can ask me anything. I have nothing to hide."

"Have you had the pig put down yet?"

"No. It's still at the Rescue."

"Good. Here. This is an injunction to keep you from taking possession of Hamlette until the animal rights people can investigate you. I've made a charge of my own. You can find out more about that later."

"You can't do that!"

Hugh grinned. "Actually, Danielle Sommars has been named the pig's guardian for now and is taking possession even as we speak."

The chief huffed but didn't get the chance to say anything else.

"As for you and the charges you've made, on behalf of myself and Miss Simms, our attorney, Michael Sommars, is suing you for libel and slander as well as defamation of character, and we have people who are starting a public campaign to have you removed from office."

"You wouldn't!"

"If I have to, Chief Cary, I'll run against you myself."

"I don't think—"

"No, you don't. If you did, you wouldn't

have done all these things to Miss Simms. I became a pawn in your game to do away with this community service. But it's not going to happen, Chief. You now have a choice. What's it going to be?"

The chief couldn't find words and stormed away.

Kendra couldn't believe it. The tide had turned, and Hugh was in the center of the waves.

An affectionate smile crossed his face. "Don't worry, lady. I'm taking care of the situation. He'll back down. He has no choice."

"I can't thank you enough."

"You don't have to. I've got to go. When you get ready, Danni has your pig."

"Thanks, Hugh."

"My pleasure." With that, he ambled away, shaking hands in the crowd as he left.

Chapter Fourteen

The next few days were a whirlwind for Kendra. The Rescue board met, reinstating her. However, there were other matters that she asked to address. Three members, including Harold Frey, resigned.

Although it was painful, the board remained calm if not friendly. Those who left did so because they did not feel they could support some of Kendra's decisions. However, they also acknowledged that she was still the best person for the position and therefore did not want to see her leave.

All in all, it was a tense two-hour meeting.

Hugh was waiting for her when she walked out of the building. "Rough day?"

She nodded, excited at the sight of him, but a nagging thought at the back of her mind wouldn't let up. "Not as bad as I thought, but still, I'd call it rough."

"Let's slip into that bistro over there. I'd like to tell you something."

She liked the slight pressure he put on the small of her back as he guided her a few doors down the street to the small, cozy restaurant. After they were seated, Hugh asked her about the meeting.

She explained that even though it wasn't the most pleasant one she'd had, it had ended well.

They each ordered coffee, and the waiter retreated.

"So all is well in the life of Kendra Simms, then?"

This was all too strange. They hadn't seen each other face-to-face since the demonstration, and although they'd talked on the phone several times, she had the terrible gut feeling that things weren't as they should be.

"I think so. Except where you're concerned, maybe."

"That's what I want to talk to you about, actually."

The waiter set their coffees in front of them.

Hugh spoke as he added cream to his. "Under the urging of Michael Sommars and Judge Cole, I've made a decision that could affect us both."

"I wasn't really sure there still was an 'us.' "

He took a sip of his drink. "I'd hoped there was. But I'm not sure what will happen when I tell you what I'm about to do."

Fear gripped her. "And what would that be?"

He cleared his throat. "I am going to run for DA."

"You've got to be kidding! After everything we've been through? Hugh, Vickie Sawyer will be all over us. She'll make our lives a living hell."

"I don't think so."

"Then you've gone crazy! She will bring me up every chance she gets. If we're still seeing each other, it'll go even worse for you."

"I want to do this. Walter used his office solely for political gain. I feel strongly about correcting that situation. I hoped you'd be supportive."

"I want to be, but I don't want to be part of a life of politics. It's so destructive. And seeing me would be your ruin."

"Think about it before you decide."

She rose from her chair. "There's nothing

to think about. In the end we're both getting what we want. You'll have your career, and I'll have my Rescue. We won, Hugh. Even if it's not meant for us to be together."

Kendra left the restaurant with a rock in her chest. She knew she loved him, but there was no chance a relationship between them could succeed now. Heavens, what had he been thinking? She got arrested every time the wind blew. Did he honestly think they could make his political office and her lifestyle work?

When she picked up Hamlette at Danni's, she told her what had happened.

"He called. I already know. Don't make him choose, Kendra. He can be a good husband and a good DA. Lots of people do it."

"Not with a wife who gets arrested just to prove a point."

"You seem to have your mind made up."

"I can't believe you would talk him into this, Danni."

"He's an honest, decent man, Kendra. Can't you share him? He'll be good for this county. He'll be good for the justice system."

"You don't get it. His entire campaign will end up being about defending me."

"That's his choice, Kendra. Take a few days

to think about it. If you can let him go, then maybe you should."

"I don't believe I let you talk me into this." Hugh pulled at his tie as if he never wore one.

"Will you calm down?" Danni waved his hands away from the tie. "You need this exposure if you're going to run for District Attorney."

"The biggest mistake I ever made was letting you talk me into that. I'm no politician."

"You can be a great DA, though. I know it."

He hoped she was right. It had been one of the biggest decisions of his life.

He sighed. So, things had worked out. The charges against him and Kendra were dropped, and both the chief and Walter were forced to resign. The best part, however, was that Vickie Sawyer left Channel Seven to pursue a career in real estate, of all things. Of course, that had a lot to do with the fact that her boss was ready to fire her.

All over a little pig.

Of course, there was Kendra. She had realized her dreams. The Rescue couldn't run without her. Some of her board resigned, and Danni filled the president's spot. Hamlette was now legally hers.

If only things could have worked out for them.

He pulled again at the tie. How in the world did he get suckered into this? Danni could talk him into anything. Now he would stand in front of an audience and be bid on like a cow in a livestock sale. Of course, he'd be carrying a sign that read RAMSEY'S RESTAURANT.

That way it wasn't really *him* that was on sale, it was the fancy steak dinner he represented.

Judge Cole was the auctioneer, as he'd been for years at this charity function. "Now, ladies and gentleman, here is the future District Attorney of White County. You'll have a chance to cast your vote for him in November, but until then you can bid on him—and the steak dinner—now. What say you?"

"A hundred dollars!"

Hugh didn't see who bid.

"Two hundred!" That was Danni. She grinned and gave him a thumbs-up.

"Three hundred!" The first woman stood and walked to the front of the audience.

Kendra!

"You can have him!" Danni joked.

"You certainly can!" Hugh took the few steps down from the podium and grabbed her into his arms. "You can have me anytime, lady."

"I'm glad. Because I had to take out a loan to bid on you."

He threw his head back and laughed. "You are impossible."

"I may be, but you'll never find a woman who loves you more than I do—or is in need of legal counsel more often."

He pulled her close and whispered into her ear, "I love you. And I can double as your lawyer, so it works out great."

Epilogue

"Now, kids, if you'll watch closely, you'll see how Grandpa Cole does this."

While the judge showed the children the magic trick for the tenth time, Hugh pulled his fiancée closer to him on the glider. They couldn't have enjoyed a better time than the judge's Fourth of July retirement party.

Joey and Hamlette lay in a corner of the deck, tuckered out from running around Danni's fenced yard.

Kendra's mother left her date's side long enough to bring drinks for her and Hugh. "So this is part of your new family, dear. I think I'm going to like it."

"You will, Mom. They're wonderful people, so you'll fit in perfectly."

"And your mother, Hugh, where is she?"

"She had a cruise planned, so I promised her you two wouldn't start on the wedding plans without her."

Vera nodded and returned to her friend.

"What do you think, lady? Think we'll be able to make a go of this?"

"I think we'd be hard pressed to give each other up. I've become addicted to you and your corny lines."

"Here's the corniest line of all. I love you. Always will. You're stuck with me."

She pulled him to her by the front of his shirt. "Good. Those are lines I want to hear forever."

"You've got it."

They sealed their deal with a kiss—and the pigs ran across their feet and out into the yard.

10/07